NAWEED ABAWI

THE LESSER MAN

"The chief characteristic of the mass man is not brutality and backwardness, but his isolation and lack of normal social relationships" – Hannah Aredent

NAWEED ABAWI

This is a work of fiction

FOREWORD

KILLING AT 'PEACE WATERS', LAS VEGAS NV

In June 2009, we were informed of a rather pungent smell wafting the corridors of residential block B in Peace Waters. A small residential area overlooking a rather peaceful river. Police were called to investigate the unknown smell and traced it back to apartment 17B. Two residents were found, stuffed in a clothing closet, with their faces decomposed, black in colour. We managed to identify these two victims, however, cannot reveal their identity. They were both male. Two gunshot wounds were inflicted upon them with their dried-up blood smeared across the walls of the dorm. We tried looking on the system for these two males but could not find them on there. We found out from their families not being able to contact them. After conducting a full search of the house, we also noticed a woman's room as well. But her body was nowhere to be found on the scene.
A receptionist was also found dead from gunshot wounds, and we assumed that the killer wanted to erase all memory of himself. The camera footage seemed to also be erased, as we couldn't find anything for that day.

As of right now, our best estimates are with the cleaning staff, as they are the only ones who have access to the room, but we have our doubts.

As for now, we must use our best guesses, but if there is an unknown killer out there, he has erased himself from all memory.

He is somewhere out there, hiding.

In the shadows.

OFFICER #8191

CONTENTS

Night   **8**

Graduation   **13**

The Job   **24**

Dead of Night   **32**

Roots   **38**

My World   *43*

The World's Revenge   **54**

Stacy.   **61**

Lost   **73**

The World's Revenge II   **80**

Lapse   *77*

Ignorant   *84*

The World's Revenge III   *94*

Desire   *113*

Tough Love	*130*
Death	*137*
The World's Revenge IV	*145*
Wanted	*157*
The Long Haul	*167*
Meredith	*174*
The World's Revenge V	*187*
The Thrill of the Hunt	*194*
The World's Revenge VI	*201*
End of the Road	*208*
The World's Revenge VII	*213*
Time	*222*
Epilogue	*231*

NIGHT
RICARDO JOAQIUN CASTILLO, 9ᵀᴴ JUNE 2013

Graduation. A day of new beginnings, and the start of a new, illustrious career. For some. For 'people' such as myself, it is a day of dread, when all you can conjure for three years is a degree that you have no passion for, let alone smart enough to be picked over the other two thousand or so applicants in the rat race for jobs. Nobody can be excited to live on cheap coffee every day, showing up just in time for a 9am shift for a job you hate to even think of, in order to provide for a 'family'. Being stuck in the system of work which chains your true desires until you 'retire'. Yet despite these logical ruminations that my mind thinks of frequently, I haven't done anything to mitigate these feelings of hapless dread. At the end of the day, I am very much situated within this 'rat race' I so passionately loathe.

If I have nothing of value to provide to society, I am immediately placed in the underclass of men. It was simple. How I wish I could tell myself that three years ago. Now, as I sleep in this shanty college dorm, with the paint chipping off the bleak white walls, with mould dissipating on the surface of the ceiling.

What was a 'man' anyways? My ancestors would be astounded to see me, an overweight twenty-three-year-old decomposing slowly through the comforts of my computers and delivery food. The comforts that western society has given me, aren't comforts at all. When one has every conceivable gratification available, they become like me, someone who doesn't deserve to be addressed as a man. No fight stored inside of him, no reason to exist in the world.

In this time, I wait. Wait for the inevitable reality, the reality that I, Ricardo Joaquin Castillo, have no hopes, aspirations or partner to accompany me. That draws my next point. Women. More complicated than the land mass calculations I did in my 'environmental planning classes'. And since a young age, I have realised no one wanted me. No one cared about me. I was the laughingstock. And it continued throughout my life. If I were a woman, at least some sad fucker like myself would go for me, but no. I had the misfortune of being placed in the rat race of men. A race I have assumed I'll never be able to win. But my sorry ass needs someone. Someone to reciprocate my primal energy towards. I was never in the mood for 'love'. I saw no point in it. Yet still, I have not been able to attain anything. No women at all. I could go on rants for days about the questions I have about life, but they don't help. People like me live in the shadows, the cracks behind the building. The columns in the newspaper that no one reads.

My stomach was in knots just thinking about the life I was about to sign up to, yet I did this to myself. There was no point in sulking about it. It had already happened anyways. Half the time I spent in college was messing about playing videogames, and ordering takeout with my weekly allowances from my parents. I couldn't get a job; I was too futile for that. I have some form of vendetta against the structure of the '9-5'. A phobia, almost. No. I couldn't sleep. I won't let myself do that. I've done absolutely nothing in college, let alone life to deserve this. No friends, no purpose, no relationship, no idea what I'm going to do after. The feeling of wailing out obscenities towards my life and my parents has taken its toll upon me. It's over now. Now the most likely case scenario will be me descending into a deep, dark void of coffee, opioids and microwave meals whilst working 7 days a week only to go on a 'holiday' for 2 weeks out of the entire year. Is this what 'education' does to people? I'm 'graduating' tomorrow. Is this meant to be an achievement? I look at the time. 5:01 A.M. I do not deserve anything. My degree in environmental planning was about to come to fruition in a couple hours.

I was too emotionally deprived of attention, that most of the time, in order to sleep I had to be hugging something, usually a body pillow, in order to go to sleep. I had stayed up tonight, until 4 am to think for once. Where does my life go after this? Do I end up like my biological father? and just wear a wife beater and work odd jobs to provide for a worthless son who doesn't show me love back? What was the meaning of life, to me at least? What did I spend 3 years doing in my so called 'masculinity'?

These questions clogged my mind as I attempted to go to sleep. I had to at least present myself well to my parents tomorrow. They haven't seen me in years, but how do I show that I at least accomplished something worthwhile here?

I'm trying to sleep, while being three hundred pounds in weight, nothing going for me, and women ignoring me and starting rumours about me like 5-year-olds. I felt like crying, as I always did when I lie in bed, without being abnormally tired. Ruminating was the worst thing I ever did. Because it's when I'm lying-in bed, is when I understand that my life is heading in directions no one would ever dream it would go. I grabbed my phone and looked at whatever, scrolling endlessly as I realised how much of a void my existence had become. But hey, at least I'm graduating tomorrow. but it's *exactly* what I did not want when I came here four years ago. Me a fucking virgin at 5:30 in the morning struggling to sleep and i'm graduating tomorrow.

I was an absolute joke of a human being in that moment, and I knew it. I didn't deserve *anything*. *Nothing*. The clarity fully set in as I overheard my roommate laughing uncontrollably. I stared, with emptiness emanating throughout my soul. I was slouched on my bed, overweight and about to enter the gruelling world of the 9-5. I can't do it. I'm too useless to do anything. It is a fickle feeling – the second after leaving school, you are down in the dumps after the pleasure subsides. I felt a tear drop from my eye as I had realised that no one ever wanted me. And most likely, no one ever will. I tried closing my eyes, but I still couldn't. Nothing would prepare me for the day ahead. I didn't want to graduate, mind you, but I knew I had to. Fuck. How do I even face my parents? I wasn't 'depressed', yet I haven't felt the feeling of 'happiness' in a while. What is happiness anyways?

    Is endless sex the answer to my problems? Is that what happiness truly is, and if it really is then I have been without meaning. *Granted*, it never did, but how the hell was I meant to attain this higher stature of autonomy? Looked at the time, 6am. No sleep. Again. And this time, it's probably the worst occasion to be sleep deprived. It's my sorry excuse of a graduation.

GRADUATION

Well, the day I dreaded has just arrived. I was truly mortified at the sight of daylight. I couldn't bear watch the sun rise as the 'song' of the birds began. Who even conceptualised the concept of 'birdsong'? to me, it always sounded like they were crying for help, if anything. Birdsong was a horrible thing, to me. It reminded me that I needed to wake up and when I do, I remind myself of everything that is wrong with me. My sorry reflection in the mirror only catalyses this feeling, but at the end of the day, I'm a sorry excuse for a soul. I turned over in my bed to pick up my phone, cracked in the centre, with the screen half dead. I let out a deep and meaningful sigh as I arose from my very short-lived slumber onto the seder floor. This was the last time I was going to see it. My bags still propped up on that sorry excuse of a desk as I looked ominously at them. Playing videogames and binging on cheap frozen pizza was my norm up until this point, but now, as I am about to move out of this run-down shithole, I realise that sooner or later, it cannot go on like this. If it does, I will be left without purpose or value.

I grabbed the bags as I see my roommate, Sal opens the door. I guess this would be the last time I see him. He was probably the opposite of what I was. I mean look at me. 'You need help carrying those bags?" He came in the room to ask me. Of course, he offered me help. He was better than me in every conceivable way. Every day of college I'd see him with a new bitch in that trap house of a bedroom. He was a smug asshole, with his damn upside-down hat, and the basketball top. He's what all those desirable females want. And exactly the type of people who would bully me during my time at high school. And as I was ruminating, he picked up the large bag, the ones with all my undersized tops and bobbleheads and walked through the dorm hallway. I followed suit, with my body pillow and computer setup.

Fuck. Fuck. Fuck. It was daylight. The very thing I was allergic to. It gets hot sometimes, but that's not what it was, it was the fact that I had just seen the essence of daylight. It wasn't for me, nor will it ever be for me.

'You aight?' - He said as I was stunned at the sight of the sun. My parents were due to pick me up, take my things back to their house, and I'll probably live there until I can attain a stable job. Hopefully by then, my mind would understand I needed work to survive. I highly doubt it, but hey. I didn't say a word as my parents were now visible in the distance. Fuck. I hadn't seen them in so long. Why am I getting emotional? Is this some new feeling I had just discovered? Nevertheless, I wasn't excited to see them in the slightest. I have been deprived of all happiness regardless of what they think, and what's funny is they are a large reason as to why I'm a sorry ass organism.

My stepfather, an admirable man, but my memories were of him always getting fired from any stable job he found, but at least he didn't beat my mother, as my biological father had done. I never did like him, my mother found him at a church she was praying at and within a couple weeks, they were married. but what a day. My parents were still rocking the raggedy ass truck, left over from my biological dad, after my mother had won the court case against him and claimed some possessions, including me. My legs were killing me as I trudged on with the luggage. 'That's your car?' the motherfucker said. He was obviously more athletically competent than me, as I held on tight to the heavy bag that I was carrying, and in visible discomfort, nodded in agreement.

He looked at it in disgust, it was a perfect reflection of my family, after all, I mean look at me. He shrugged his shoulders as he walked towards it. There they were. My parents didn't like me either, specifically my stepfather, even though I wouldn't expect him to care, me not being the 'biological son' and all. I mean I would hate me too, if I were in his position.

'You must be the roommate' Both of my parents said in broken English.

'Uh, yeah' the smug motherfucker replied.

'I'll just, uh leave this with you if that's okay' – he said as he walked off. He wanted to escape, didn't he? Who wouldn't after seeing my parents? His basketball top swayed in the hot sun as I stood there, awkwardly looking.

'We are so proud of you son', said my 'father', he was fatter than me, however, looking as smart as I've ever seen him. He was always the kind to wear tank tops and slippers but looks like he could put some effort into wearing a suit, with an unknown stain brandished upon it. I looked at him in disgust, in truth, I didn't like it. but who am I to complain anyways, I wasn't exactly the best looking *'man'* either? I say 'man' lightly because, after what happens most nights, I think it's universal that I do not *deserve* to be addressed as a man, let alone be acknowledged as an imposing figure. My mother, around the same weight, looked at me with an aura of disgust and distain, possibly to reciprocate the energy I was giving my father. We stood awkwardly and talked, for a little while, I was still in my fucking PJs, but the basketball top fucker had left.

'The graduation is in a couple hours son; you best get ready'. He said it with some excitement rather than being drowned out, as I remember him being. I'd never heard my stepfather speak to me like this before. He personally always wanted a strong, masculine son, but I'm none of those things, plus I did not get any chances to bond with him since I was older when he and my mother decided to get married. but I guess the little success in graduating from college swayed his mind just that little bit, and considering that he was a driving force as to why I decided to become an 'environmental planner', he must have been that much more proud.

'Uh, thanks guys, I really appreciate it'
I said as I gawked at the raggedy mess of a truck, they put my precious belongings in. I wanted to say something, but I left it be, not being inside a locked bedroom really did take a toll on my mind. I couldn't go a second without it, I needed it. I really did.

Fuck me. I walked back, that was already enough exercise for me for the day at least, I thought as I opened the door back into the shithole I'd be looking at for the last time. I opened my room door and whacked on some 'formal clothes' I had been saving simply for this occasion. I hated the way the clothes felt tight, pressed against my sorry excuse of a body. I was thinking of wearing a leather jacket or something, but I had nothing else, and besides I'll be wearing that black gown or whatever over it. I wore my shoes, that were creased and stained from years of wear and tear, and took a good long stare at the room I had spent 3 years of my sorry life living in. What a waste. I immediately withdrew from this compound of degeneracy and quickly had one last look at everything. Went into the bathroom. Mould-stained tiles still cascading off the walls with leftover soap stored within the shower. Looked in the mirror. Look at me. I am a sorry ass, raggedy fuck. My hair was a greasy mess, long and filled to the brim with dandruff. The last time I had a haircut was also the last time I felt any sort of confidence. Confidence was something I couldn't have. The world did not allow it. It was almost as if the saplings of life had pulled themselves from underneath me, leaving exposed the dusty and reckless roots of the tree. It's been like that for a while. Fuck. I'm thinking too much. I took one last glance at the shower I never used. Not even this morning, a day in which I'm supposed to look my 'smartest'. Hey, I don't even know half the 'professors' who taught me. I really am a nobody – yet I'm going to be graduating.

As I was sitting on the bed, I caught a whiff of my body odours I didn't bother cleaning. I felt a sense of animalistic intent, almost as if I wanted to do something. I was too afraid to admit it. The greatest human enemy is the mind. Can't be true, can it?

No.

There is no way I'm about to do this.

I'm going to be graduating.

My parents are literally waiting for my sorry ass to get 'ready'.

What even is getting 'ready'? having a shower? Because clearly, I'm not taking one.

My breathing intensified, I tried to shut down the urges, I needed to.

Do I even have any self-control?

No, no no. My mind was in a constant battle now, a race against time to stop my urges. It started asking questions.

It started, talking to me?

I could feel sweat trickle down my sorry excuse for a forehead, acne perched up against the pores on my forehead, my thick face was now acting as a barrier against this mess.

Don't do it.

Don't do it.

Fuck.

I did it. 'Every fucking time' I kept repeating, as if it were some twisted mantra. My fingertips moving constantly as I was coming to terms with what I had done. I had no reason to, but something came over me. Something I simply, could not control. My teeth bore a degree of weight upon me as I kept chattering. My confidence was ruined from this endeavour, again, not that I had any to even begin with. Now I've got to face my parents, for this fucking graduation. Why have I done this? Did I need to? Fuck no.

Can't be caught again.

2:15 P.M.

Fuck.

I arose from this absolute state I found myself in and walked out of the room. This was the last time I'd see it. I got out and turned off the light. Did I even clean the grime out of my nails? Too late anyways, all my shit was left back in that insult of a truck, the last remanent of my biological father.

"Well I guess this is goodbye" I say to my room, the same place I've done unimaginable things in, but nevertheless, it was emotional seeing the place for what was, the last time.

And as I left this dorm, I realised that the meaning of life, for me was nothing. People go to college to find their purpose, *fuel* the passion that will lead on to their career. But I'm not ready. Environmental planning? Seriously? I haven't even stepped a foot outside other than get food to fuel my ever-increasing body size. Well, I never really sought purpose in the first place, so I guess I had it coming. How purposeful would a specimen such as me be anyways? Fuck it's hot. The blast of heat surprised me again as I stepped out. Brisked past the stairs and made my way out of the dorm complex for the final time. Block 209 was written on the wall next to the complex in gold paint that was beginning to wear, and the door was cracking at the seams. And with that, I made my way to my parents' 'truck'. I am about to graduate in front of hundreds of people I barely even made a connection with in the first place. This was not how I envisioned the day going, let alone even envisioning it in the first place. I hate working. I hate the idea of getting a 'graduate job'. I won't do it. Yet I need to find some purpose in this life, and not be a burden, as I always have been. This is the 'real world' after all. Plus, my parents probably won't let me stay in their house for long, I need to find some 'stability', whatever that may mean.

The car now pulled up to the long stretch of road with the college hall. A guy approached us as my 'father' pulls down the window of the shitty truck. The guy looked tall; you could smell his masculine fragrance from the back where my sorry ass was sitting. Legs stretched and all, breathing heavily from the lack of AC in this thing. He looks at me and says – "You need to put on your gown in there", and points to a tent with girls on the outside of it. I nod in agreement, I don't use words often, and he struts away, I could see the biceps through his thin white shirt as he kept walking, with an aura of confidence about him, something I was certainly lacking. I open the shitty door and attempt to get out. My peripheral vision suddenly realised the girls staring at my presence. Even I would. Look at the state of me. I hadn't caught sight of any females in the past few months, so this was certainly something new. *Fuck.* They notice me walking towards this tent and stifle their laughs, as if I were to do anything. As I walk past, they also now caught sight of my fucking tight shirt and creased black trousers, with stains of degeneracy left upon it.

They didn't even want to laugh anymore.

I cringed as I walked past and into this 'changing tent' and ran into a plus sized woman, not my size but surely insecure enough to know that she shouldn't probably laugh. But she was in my league. Fuck. I looked at her and decided the best option was to stick my tongue out, just that little bit, maybe to show her that I was interested. I completely forgot how the opposite gender would perceive me, judging from the fact that I hadn't interacted with them in a while. But it backfired, as always as she creates one of the worst faces, I've probably ever seen. It was elements of disgust mixed with shock with a hint of danger.

"Excuse me sir?"

Well, that didn't go as planned. Yet another painfully sorry attempt at trying to get women. Why do I even do this to myself? She handed me the 'gown' as she looked away whilst doing it. Am I really that hideous? I quickly retreat into another one of these 'changing tents' and looked at the gown for a second, I've just fucked up another conversation with a woman. Again. I took a glance at the tag. It had 'XXL' emblazoned in red upon it. Probably for the best. As I wore it, I felt the cheap material press against my 'chest', constantly trying to break away from what I had just done to that woman. What the actual hell was I wearing, and *why* was I? I don't deserve it. My 'degree' is too futile for this. The mirror barely stood on the edge of this shitty 'tent', but my beer belly was on full show to any victim that dared to even look at me. I ripped that 'XXL' tag off the cloak and opened the zip up to get out of there.

There, my parents stood, my stepfather wearing his 3-piece suit, the same one he wore to his wedding with my mother. He was *shocked* to see me like this.

"We are proud of you son, we really are"

God. That was the 3rd time he's said that. Not that I will complain, I just felt weird seeing him address me like that. And he's never addressed me as 'son'. That statement was untrue, I never accepted him as my father in the first place. He pointed to the place they had to be sitting and left me on my way. I looked in the direction of where I was meant to go, and shit. My legs began to disintegrate as I attempted to walk over to the place everyone would be sitting.

The jocks confidently walked up to their seats as I began to wait. I had to wait, there was no way I'd let anybody look at me walking like an idiot, I hardly know anybody there.

Well looks like I *have* to go in.

I was the last one to walk up, and as I do, I'm stopped by a shorter looking male with flyers in his hands.

"Afterparty is at 6, don't forget".

An afterparty?

The last time I went to a party didn't go over too well anyways, I was and never will be the type. After the nightmare that had just transpired, I would rather curl up in a ball and forget my existence.

"Yeah, uh thanks" – as I took the flyer, it had men and women being degenerates with alcohol flying in the air. Fucking hell. I was so deprived of female attention, yet I had no confidence. I tried not to second guess it anyways. I'm not going. It isn't for me. I'm not cut out for this absolute bullshit.

THE JOB

THE LESSER MAN

RICARDO JOAQIUN CASTILLO, 17ᵀᴴ JULY 2013

It seems I have just graduated. I didn't know whether to cry, to laugh or just drown my sorrows. Seeing everyone feeling fulfilled in some shape or form didn't help things either, as I soon found myself in a bar which was a ten-minute walk away from where I had graduated. I felt more at home here, seeing men who had their palms in their faces, drinking endlessly until being kicked out, whilst being black out drunk. I downed a couple, before planting my face onto the wooden tabletop. I couldn't help but feel my life had been wasted, for alcohol was only a temporary fix for my never-ending list of problems. Being alone was a harsh reality I needed to adapt to. My suffering had only been heightened by my presence at this bar. I took a quick glance at the man next to me with his hands in his palms. He was being asked to leave by the bartender, but just like everyone else who came here, he refused to do so. I couldn't blame him anyways, he looked defeated; as if someone had taken every ounce of happiness away from his life. I knew that men struggled. I had experienced it myself. But seeing all these men gathered here, told me everything I needed to know about the bitter dynamics between the genders. The bar was about to close, it was almost 3. I downed a couple more before I tried to get up and leave. I stayed sat down there, however. I felt like I had let my parents down, even though I had just 'graduated' from college. The luminescent walls in the corner of the room became blurrier as I stopped and looked at them. I felt a certain pain when I kept that stare, but I couldn't stop looking. It was the only ray of light in a room full of darkness.

darkness. I pulled out the flyer from my pockets again. The image of men and women partying didn't strike my fancy, but I knew it was the only way to become 'social' in this desolate world. I knew that degenerates got the most attention and social interaction, especially with women. I chucked the flyer on the ground, before downing a little more of my drink. I had a couple bucks, and kept asking for more. I wouldn't stop until I fell completely unconscious, until my soul felt as if it would implode and give me amnesia, to make me forget the lowlife I really was. I drank more, until I caught sight of a man sitting next to me from the corner of my eye.

"Is this yours?" he said.

I finally spun my head around to get a good look at him. He was bigger than I was, yet similar. His hair was dishevelled alongside his face, which was covered in some weird scars alongside his facial features. He looked like the type I would feel sorry for in my teenage years, but as I am now older, I realised I am exactly the type to feel sorry for. He had the flyer I had just carelessly tossed in his hand and started reading it.

"You just graduated?" he said, whilst still reading the flyer, with degenerates plastered all along the front. "Why aren't you celebrating?"

I let out a small chuckle before finishing my third drink of the night. "There's nothing to be excited about. Life only goes downhill from here." I said, whilst looking away from him. "I have nothing to look forward to". It felt relieving to get those words out, as I had been meaning to tell someone the extent of my sorrows.

The man, who looked older than I was, got out his wallet and asked the bartender for a drink. He downed a shot and let out a sigh.

"Listen, I don't know you, but what I do understand is your problems" he said, as he looked directly into my eyes. "I've felt useless all my life."

They weren't exactly the most optimistic words I had heard.

"I'm guessing you don't exactly strike a chord with the 'ladies' either?" he said, in a snarky, sarcastic manner.

It felt obvious that I couldn't get women, from my appearance. But it didn't seem like he did the same either.

"Well, not really" I replied.

"Those bitches never learn" he said. "Women never go for guys like us unfortunately. And there's a big chance you won't feel the touch of a woman" he said. "Son, I've tried and failed countless times, often failing in horrific fashion. Those bitches have a flawed mindset. Much less intelligent than you and I".

I didn't know exactly what to think upon hearing what he had just said. It seemed like he hated women, to an extent I had never heard of personally. I never did hate women myself, despite being ridiculed and mocked by them every waking second. I could understand where this man was coming from, as he looked to be in a similar predicament as me.

"What's your name anyways?" he said, as he asked the bartender for one more drink. It seemed like he wanted to get drunk.

"Ricardo. Ricardo Joaquin Castillo". I said, as I was moving my empty drink glass around the table.

"The names Remi. Remi Palludan"

He downed his drink as he said it.

I never did intend to find 'friends' whilst at the bar, but the way we conversed for the next few minutes gave me a sense of fulfilment I hadn't experienced before. He felt like someone who finally understood me and didn't give mindless robotic responses to my dilemmas.

He carried on drinking through the night, as I was slumped in the chair after downing one too many. Those childhood memories had now become a nightmare as I longed for that sense of freedom I now cannot experience.

Remi had now become drunk from constantly downing huge amounts of alcohol at the bar. I could see that a girl with black hair had now sat a couple seats away from us, and despite Remi's obvious hatred for women, he looked at her with a deep lust in his eyes. I could also see that she was appealing, with her black corset and exposed legs. Remi also shared the same sentiment and proceeded to move closer to her. He was clearly finished from the constant drinking, and drunkenly moved closer.

He proceeded to caress her exposed legs and by the looks of it, didn't utter a word before or after he attempted it. His stature loomed over her like a dark cloud, before eventually casting itself upon her.

"You fucking pervert" she screamed. "Get the fuck off me", she said as she signalled for him to be removed. The security swiftly jumped in, and despite his large size, grabbed him and forced his drunk self out.

I decided to leave as well, following Remi out of the place.

As he was being dragged out, he started squirming in the security officer's grasp.

"You're just like that bitch Meredith you fucking whore" he said as he was being thrusted and forced out. His pleasure had stopped right there as he disappeared from my blurred vision. I followed him out, as he tried to navigate the dead of night.

"It was nice meeting you" I said, as he struggled to stay upright.

"Keep in touch, I want to meet you again" he replied, to which I nodded and let him resume his drunk walk. I wasn't much better, stumbling across the sidewalk every single step. That two-hour conversation was eye opening, but I now needed to make it back to my parents' abode in Oakland, to spend a couple weeks before they expect me to get a job. My stepfather isn't the most optimistic of my abilities, nor has he ever been. For as long as I could remember, he never showed me any affection in the way a 'father' would do. He never saw any real potential in me either. My size and overall lack of ambition was a large indicator of this.

As I stared in the night sky, at the luminescent moon, casting a spell over the ground below, its rays captivated me as I walked toward the station, or so I had hoped.

I walked through the night, with no real sense of direction as I only saw the blurry reflections of lights on cars and streetlights. I knew that I was close to blacking out, as I continued my journey through the deviant night. I was all too familiar with the scenes of couples making out in the dead streets, and the taxi drivers reeling drunken dogs into their vehicles. The deviance of the night was something I now found solace in. I found a chair sitting upright from a closed restaurant and turned it around. I decided to sit for a bit, and take in the surroundings of the night, and also to recapture my footing before setting off. To my shock, I saw Remi, slumped in the middle of the sidewalk, unable to get up. I quickly rushed to his aid and pulled him up.

"You alright?" I said, as I struggled to pull his abnormally large weight up.

"Fuck that whore Meredith, fuck her" he said in a soft tone as he arose from the sidewalk.

I was confused as to who 'Meredith' was, as he kept saying her name without purpose.

A group of men looked ominously towards us, with hatred in their eyes.

"You fucking pervert" they screamed. Obviously indicated at Remi, as they looked him in the eye as they were saying it. I'm guessing Meredith was the girl he touched.

"Well, Remi you do know it's a crime to touch women like that" I said to him. He clearly wasn't listening, but it was worth a shot.

"Ricardo, do you really think I care? I fucking hate those whores. They don't deserve a second of human time" he said, whilst looking away from me.

"Let me help you walk" I said as I put his arm around my shoulder. He came to the bar after me yet was incredibly more drunk than I was.

"Fuck, I appreciate it Ricardo" he said, as he struggled to even lay a foot on the sidewalk.

The men continued to stare at us, with a feeling of disgust as I was the one helping Remi navigate the dead of night.

Remi had done something wrong, yet he showed no remorse for the actions he had committed. To me, he seemed like a man incredibly frustrated with life, a man who could not bear to see others achieve their sexual desire. It sounded a lot like my tragic life thus far. He continued to murmur odd phrases continuously as I trudged him forward. He kept uttering the name, 'Meredith' as I dragged him through the streets.

"So, where do you want to go?" I said, for the first time after dragging him along the sidewalk.

"Just take me to that motel up front" he said, struggling to even utter the words from his mouth.

I could see one up front, and I continued to drag him, as if he were a dead body. His arms and torso were harbours of fat, collected harshly in a lump on his side. His body wasn't something to be proud of, as I carried him through the harsh San Francisco night. His drunk state was far worse than others I had seen, even myself. It was as if his body had shut off completely, as he now relied solely on my physical strength to get him through.

"Remi?" I said, trying to get him to wake up.

"Oh shit". He now woke up and took some weight off my shoulders. "Thanks man". He said. "Keep in touch, I'll speak to you soon". He exclaimed, as he made his way inside the motel.

I still had enough time to make it back to Oakland, as the time was now 4 in the morning. I couldn't spend another night in this degenerate shithole. I wasn't cut out for it.

Yet I was left to contemplate who this 'Meredith' was that he kept talking about. Despite the long conversation we had, he was still an enigmatic individual. One that could possibly add a little spice to my bland life.

DEAD OF NIGHT

I hopped on a train going to Oakland and found an empty seat. The train was for once, surprisingly empty.

The only other person on this train was a woman, didn't look a day above 30, with neat, straightened hair and glasses. Her female self looked untouched in her beauty, and her hands were intricately delicate, exactly like that woman back at the graduation. Her She was attractive, but I still hadn't gotten over what that woman had said to me back on campus, so I tried to concentrate on my phone. She looked way out of my 'league' anyways. They all do that. I fixed up my glasses and waited as the train ran through the stations. Feeling the emptiness and lifeless void of the train, with the only thing accompanying me being the artificial female voice of the train system.

It approached a standstill, and as I was rubbing an eye, I hear a faint voice: "Hey beautiful."

I widened my eyes and opened them only to see a man, thin as paper, wearing a bandana that looked like it could fall off the top of his face, sporting the spikiest hair I have ever seen. You could almost see the bones through his thin and scaly arms. He looked coked out of his mind; you could see it in his eyes. They looked a bloodshot red. With the small veins in his eyes poking out from within. His posture resembled that of a hunchback; he was struggling to walk, or even stand straight.

But he was talking to that pretty girl across from me.

"I saw you from across the station and I really just want to fuck you if I'm being honest,

Wow. He really went straight to the point. Well, she had to say something. And she did. She had headphones on, and took them off, she was in shock of what had just been said to her.

With her shocked expression visible from all areas of her face, she replied "Sorry, I'm not interested". Should have been the signal for this guy to stop, right?

But just from his demeanour, you could probably tell what kind of person he was. He was not going to take no for an answer. I could feel myself grasping the certificate in my hand more as I began to sweat more profusely. I would make fists when I would be stressed. It's almost as if I knew what he was going to do next. Surely from all the years of being bullied I could feel an imminent sense of danger from this guy, I don't know about the woman, but I certainly could sense it.

"Come on miss, you are the most beautiful, most grand, most smart woman I've ever seen. Come on. Please."

Sounds like he was desperate. He was slurring his words, it gradually got worse every time he spoke. He was just pulling words out of his ass at this point. My eyes remained fixated on my phone. I didn't want this to boil over into my business. This guy was on drugs, you never know what can happen.

His facial expression changed. He looked desperately mad now. The train opened its doors, yet no one came in. And when it departed again, he resumed his harassment.

"Bitch. I'm not fucking playing." He said, as he ran his fingers through the spikes on his hair. His hands were going all over the place. He really was intoxicated out of his mind. The woman looked visibly distressed, and she turns to me. I for one, had never seen something so enigmatic before.

Fuck. Fuck. Shit. I had no choice now but to look up from my phone. This guy was getting restless. My heartbeat, going in circles, just wanted to leave. I needed to reach Oakland.

She started to breathe heavily, and this guy started banging the wall of the train. The woman cowered in fear as he relentlessly shook the train with his veiny, skinny hands.

"You fucking bitch. This is my fucking problem with all of you." He started chanting. "Women are so fucking complicated. Especially fucking you". He says with a senile facial expression. Then, it happened. The banging on the walls stopped. I looked up, had he gone? No. It was far worse. He directed his hand somewhere else. , he struck her in the face. Totally unprovoked. The woman screamed for help.

"That's right, bitch, you fucking whore"

"You fucking deserve it; you fucking deserve it"

His hands were in constant motion. And it didn't help that there was no one in the carriage. Me? You must be joking. Even though I could probably square up to this guy, there was something about him, his aura which overpowered mine. Even though this guy was a twig, I couldn't. I just couldn't.

"You wanna fuck now, huh? Bitch?" She cowered in fear before him. I felt my hand. It was shaking. My breathing, started to go up. The man wouldn't stop. What are you doing? My brain kept on

34

saying to me repeatedly. Help her. Help her. Help her. It kept repeating in my mind. Why are you just sitting there? What are you doing?

"All you guys fucking want is some fucking attention, right bitch?" he kept repeating. My legs were still set in stone. I couldn't do shit. The nerve endings in my feet were numbed. Completely silent. My father used to hit my mother. It was normal, was a thought that came amongst many thoughts in my mind. But the screams, the pleas for help in that circumstance, was it normal? My head sunk into my hands, as she was relentlessly attempting to get away. Help her. Help her. Help her. But no. I'm too much of a pussy for that. She sounded like she was getting beaten up badly. It cast my mind back to when I got beat back in high school, pinned up against the lockers and hell rained down on me. I could almost sense the rumble on my nose, with blood dripping down. Being pressed up against the metal, feeling that pain as I sat there after, understanding that my life has no value. This woman must be going through the same thing. The man didn't stop.

Until he did. He finally got off at the next, empty station and directed a spit at her.

"You are a fucking whore, don't forget" – he said, as he was slurring his words immensely. He couldn't even walk straight. He was really out of his mind.

She was breathing, heavily. The makeup she had used dripped off her cheek. Her glasses were shattered. And there my sorry ass was, refusing to even do anything.

She grabbed her purse, checked that everything was still in it, it was. So you're telling me a guy just wanted to assault a woman on a train? He didn't do anything else.

I looked around, and the woman, in all her fragility, looked at me. We made eye contact, and she looked directly at me, as if she wanted to kill me.

She looked at me and said: "You don't deserve to be called a man. Men wouldn't let that happen". I looked at her, frozen and amazed at her face. What happened was so random, I couldn't compute the fact that she had just been beaten very badly. I didn't know what to say, She took the words right out of my mouth. "You looked at someone hitting me, raining hell on me, you looked, and you didn't do shit". Her voice was breaking as she let it all out, her screams had been ripped right out of her. "I hope this happens to your loved one, if you even have any". She didn't need to say it this way. I was already embarrassed as it is. Plus, I won't be getting a 'loved one' who is female any time soon, and after this, I doubt I could get one.

She was clearly distressed; I could see it in her eyes, but who wouldn't be?

"I mean look at me. You shouldn't rely on a person like me, who can't even fend off against a fly."

I just let it out.

She looked at me, and probably understood where I was coming from. I wasn't the ideal person to defend anybody.

"Then kill yourself. You aren't a man." She frantically reached for a tissue in her bag. She wasn't robbed, either. But she took the words right out of my mouth, I did contemplate killing myself, numerous times. She gave me a stare as she got off the train, her face was still bloodied. She really had no filter. I guess that's what happens when you get beat up on a train. I've been in that situation before, but I've never been complimented before someone rains hell all over me. My stop wasn't far behind, either. My legs still felt like jelly, but the way that man imposed himself on that woman, was to me, crazy. I was bigger than that crackhead. He was a skinny fucker, but what was even more bizarre, was that he didn't even sexually assault her. I mean I would probably get hard if he did, I'll be brutally honest, but he didn't. Maybe it's because she didn't show passion. Passion is what it is all about. As I trudged out of that carriage, a chain of thought occurred to me. Was this masculinity? Did that women want me to beat that man up only based on the sole purpose of my non-existent 'masculinity'. I am old enough now to realise, that this was a survival. A survival of the fittest. Men unlike women, possess primal instincts. I for one, fall into the very bottom of this. I was lesser than a rat to women. What a fucking cruel world we live in. I grabbed my certificate, the only thing in my hand, checked I had everything, and got off the train. I was in Oakland.

ROOTS

Well, I'm back home. I approached the driveway, with the rusted truck parked illegally on the curb. We never did get our own 'driveway' mainly because there wasn't enough space where our house was. I walked on the road I always used to play on, the potholes still etched exactly where I remember them. And many times, on this road, I was bullied by the other kids around the neighbourhood. This was the same road I used to ride my hand me down BMX bike from my aunt, until I got bullied by some kids calling me 'too fat' to ride a bike and had it stolen off me. The rapid excitement the day I had got it, to being fat shamed, beat up and it being taken away from me only hours later. The only question I really had at that time was 'why me'. The memories here were a mixed bag for me. How could I feel nostalgic about a place that had troubled me for so long?

I looked around. It looked like the neighbour's son was still living in their house. I could tell by the screams of him and his mother, usually arguing in Spanish, but when he was very angry, he would often switch to speaking English, so his mother wouldn't understand him properly. I remember him cornering me as I was coming back home from a particularly shitty day at high school and beating me to a pulp after realising, I lived on the same street. I was always the target at high school, mainly because the 'jocks' wanted to prove how tough they were by beating up a plus sized, fat kid. I never did put up much of a fight though, mainly because I always felt inferior. As they were having their screaming match, I walked up to the house. Nothing had changed since I had last been here 4 years ago. The door was still that pale, washed-out blue with the doorbell unable to function. I just knocked the door and felt a rumble coming from the house. I stood back just a bit. As a child, I would peek through the little hole, to see if my father was back home yet, because when he was at home, there was always that risk he would be in a bad mood and beat me and my mother up. The door opened, and my mother came out, surprised.

"You're home early" she said in Spanish. It was in a sarcastic manner, but something told me she was serious, because it was anything but 'early'.

I guess she expected me to be at this 'party' after the graduation, but after what Remi had done to that woman in the bar and that girl on the train, the last thing I want is to interact with women.

"Yeah, the party was fun" as I ignored her questions about where I had been.

It seemed believable enough to my mother, so she just about accepted it. I looked around the house. Not much had changed since I had last left. My parents had become too old to really renovate anything, anyways. The pictures were still from the 90s, some of them washed out, and the frames chipping off the cheap gold paint. The smell of the old lavender room spray that my mother always used to mask the smell of my father's chain-smoking habit in the living room, still prevalent within my nostrils as soon as I walked in.

"So is my stuff in my room?" I said as I caught the door to my room in my peripheral. She nodded in agreement, as I walked toward the door. This was my retreat every time things became heated between my parents, unless I wanted to be caught by my father's drunken rampages, I had to go in here. The doorknob was still discoloured as

I opened it to reveal my old room. My computer setup was still there, which was a good thing, but hadn't been plugged in. my suitcases were scattered across the bed and the posters were lying on the floor. I took a second to memorise where the outlets were again and started assembling my computer setup. The desk hadn't changed, still covered in dust, and a faint brown, with my belongings on top of it. The desk? Where do I even begin? The same desk I used to express my love to my crush back when I was 6. I didn't have the confidence to tell her in person, so I decided back then, to write what I called, a 'confession' letter, and expressed my feelings to her. I wish I would've known that a fat Spanish kid is probably not most of the girls' type, but I was stupid and lovesick, so I went for it. And to this day, the decision to give it to her in class still haunts me. I passed her the note, and well, what followed haunted me for the rest of my years in elementary school. She decided to pass it around, and soon enough, I became the laughingstock of the whole school, up until I left. The note became a symbol, an incentive for kids to bully the hell out of me because I was labelled as the school's 'pervert', someone to be feared and gave a reason for the jocks to beat me up. After that day, I swore to myself I would never do such a thing again. In fact, it was my fault that I even thought of 'loving' someone in the first place. It's all a competition. A survival of the fittest. I could not comprehend it at the time, but it was. What stupidity to even assume I was desirable, in the larger race of masculine competition.

So, every time I see this desk, it reminds me of my stupidity. The start of my fatal quest of female attention, that I still haven't conquered and most likely won't. So, when Remi told me what the reality was, honestly, I wasn't even surprised. Now my PC setup was on, just as I had left it in my college dorm. I cleared a bit of dust off the screen and turned it on. Whilst it was getting ready, I figured it would be a good time for me to change my clothing, and so I did, grabbing the big blue suitcase from on top of my bed. My bed hadn't changed. The only thing that did was the bedding, but the thing was still ridged in from the one time I busted too hard and subsequently broke the springs from underneath it. I was a fat shit, so it was inevitable.

Decided to wear those PJs from the night before and just crash for the night. I yanked my phone out of my pocket and set it down on the desk next to my bed.

   I'm guessing my mother could tell that I had been drinking heavily after the graduation, as even I could smell the alcohol on my person as I went to sleep. I wish I could have told her that I drank with 'friends' at the party, but, I was slumped over accepting the fact that I was a failure, whilst downing a multitude of different alcoholic drinks.

I had to grab something, because I think I will be scrolling here for a long while even though it was the dead of night. So, I presented myself in the kitchen. It was 11p.m, but my parents were asleep. They always love to sleep at the earliest hours of the night, so this was perfect. The Cheetos were still kept in the same cupboard I always used to steal them from. They were the main reason I was so enlarged and fat out of my mind. They were just too good to surpass for anything. So, I grabbed one, closed the cupboard, and walked back to my room. I locked the door. It felt as if I was about to start beating, but no. I needed to sleep, as I could not bear to stay awake a minute longer, to remind me of what had transpired on my dreaded graduation day.

MY WORLD

I must have been out cold for a while, as I woke up at around 2 in the afternoon. I opened my phone to a magnitude of missed calls, mostly from an unknown number. The feeling of being hungover is something I cannot physically escape from. My joints felt disconnected from my body, and my head was certainly not clear. I immediately got a call again from the same number. Usually, I would not answer these types of calls, but since I was heavily hungover, I mistakenly accepted that call.

"Hello?" I said, in a rather disgruntled and disjointed voice.

"Ricardo? It's Remi, Remi Palludan"

He sounded like he was on edge. But I couldn't complain after the antics he performed last night.

"The guy from yesterday?" I asked yet knowing the answer.

"Yes, yes it's the same guy" he said, as he sounded like he was going to burst. "Hey, listen I appreciate what you did for me last night. I don't know how I would have gotten home myself" he said, in a relieved tone. "I'm usually cranky and violent when I am drunk. So I really do appreciate it"

"No problem, I liked your company" I said back.

"Listen, meet me behind the strip club near the train station. I feel like simply expressing my gratitude for what you did wasn't enough. I want to give you something"

It sounded like a nice gesture, but all I did was drag his drunken self from point A to point B.

Yet, I wanted to see him again. I hadn't felt proper friendship in a good while.

I decided to meet him, and see what this 'return in gratitude' really was. It was against my better judgement, but I had nothing of worth to do anyways. I knew that I was on a time schedule at this house, as my stepfather would not let me live in the house forever. I didn't think I wanted a 'job' this soon, but it seems that's what my parents wanted.

The club he asked me to go to was in a shady area, as all strip clubs are. It seemed like he was desperate for some female attention, but never got any. It was quite like my own dilemmas. That's probably why I felt such a strong connection with him in the first place. I would usually eat when I was hungover, as I did when I stayed at that college dorm. I decided to unpack whilst I was here, since I had only just crashed onto bed last night.

My parents had brought my large suitcase back home, and I placed it onto my bed, before unfastening the straps inside of it. My clothes and personal belongings were stuffed inside, I wasn't the type to 'fold' my clothes anyways. Hell, I didn't even 'iron' anything whilst I was there. I didn't even have the energy to get up and leave my room. Who would after carrying a 200lb man through the dark, sullen streets at night whilst being drunk themselves.

I brought home a Michael Jackson 'Bad' poster. It had been there since I had moved in, I was guessing the last guy in that dorm didn't want to keep it and was ignorant, so I ended up bringing it home with me. I grabbed everything I could from that dorm, and I ended up taking some things that I wouldn't.

I was too hungover for this anyway. I couldn't move my hands, let alone get up safely. I assumed this was how my life was going to play out now. Getting drunk every single night and coming home to sleep until the late hours of the afternoon. Why did Remi want to go and visit a strip club? It was no secret I was a virgin, and I wanted to lose that virginity, fast. I had never hoped for it to be lost to a prostitute or at a brothel. I wanted real companionship. Someone who could see eye to eye with me, understand me, and be with me for the rest of time. I only saw sexual relations as a by-product of having someone to love.

My room had not changed that much since I last inhabited it. The white walls were still the same, with the thin walls bending every time you would knock on them. I was still hungover; the feeling would usually subside by now. But yesterday was not anything normal. The feeling of knowing your fate at an age like mine would cause anyone to go insane and drink until you lost the ability to think rationally. I didn't get a good chance to look at my room when I initially went in, mainly because I was blacked out the entire time. I could say I missed having my parents around, specifically my mother, as I knew she was one of the most caring individuals I knew. The feeling of care was something I had not experienced in a while. I would hope that having someone who genuinely cares for you would ease the pain I had in my heart for a while. Hence why I most likely felt at ease when Remi spoke to me.

I hoped my problems with women would be over, but I had hoped that ever since I was the tender age of 16. They never did stop. I was always mocked and heckled for even attempting to step into this realm.

I could hear my stepfather from the other room, his voice was very distinct, I heard it all the time in my nightmares. His voice was something I learned to fear, and respect in a twisted manner. I decided to finish unpacking, even though I hadn't really finished emptying my belongings.

I eventually smelled cooking. It's been a while since someone has cooked for me, or even being around the presence of 'freshly' cooked food. I've always been the type to either order delivery or whack something in the oven in my shitty college dorm. But this, this felt nostalgic, and for once in a good way. It gave me memories of a Saturday morning in which my mother would cook enormous spreads, which I believe was the main contribution to my weight, but they were a thing of beauty. Even after being fat shamed relentlessly at school, I would still pig out at whatever my mother would cook for breakfast. I could feel the smell wafting from the main room, and before I made an advance I checked my phone, the time was 3PM. Nevertheless, I got up and fixed my glasses upon myself.
I arose from the bed, it had served me well the entire night, better than I thought it would, and I walked into the living space. My mother, just as she had during my childhood, stood there, preparing it.

"You know It's been a while since we have eaten together as a family" she said as she looked at me, a smile brandished upon her face, penetrating all her wrinkles. I looked at her and returned the smile. "It has been a while" I said, as I took a seat at the table. My fat folds stretched the entire length of the seat and pressed hard against the cheap leather of the wooden framed chair. My mother presented me the plate. It was the usual I had always eaten. Eggs. But my mother would make them some odd type of way, a way I couldn't replicate in my own dorm. There was a lot, potentially because she knew that I would inhale food. And I did. This time was no different, possibly because I had not eaten such things in a long while. I felt my familiar sense of nostalgia as I finished it, and my mother cleared the plates. These experiences were one of the few things I ought to have savoured in my childhood, mainly because the rest of my childhood was not that great of an experience.

What did I do with the rest of the day? I have never awoken this early for as long as I could remember.

I took some time to digest what had happened yesterday. It was probably one of the most event filled days of my life in the last four years. It was a day that changed me, but at what cost? Depending on what happens after this, I will begin to take a very different trajectory. I decided to log on to my PC, I didn't feel like doing anything worthwhile today, except for getting back on that train to where this club is. I really didn't feel like doing it, but I was afraid of the so called 'consequences' if I didn't.

I decided, for once to take a shower, mainly because I had now got a knack for re-living my childhood experiences after that breakfast. Plus, as I was sleeping last night, I could feel the sweat accumulating all across me, so I believed it was the best option.

I asked my mother where the towels were, and she directed me to them. I grabbed some 'fresh' clothing and walked into the bathroom.

I waited for my father to finish up and entered after him. The bathroom was a steam ridden hellhole now, the steam engulfed me, as all I could see was a blurry rendition of myself in the mirror, and the smells of Old Spice cascaded throughout, as if I was in some new, twisted reality. I began to take off my clothes in frantic fashion. I wasn't used to this. The concept of taking a shower. I wiped the steam-stained mirror to see myself properly. The pores in my skin, the discolouring of my neck areas and the folds tucked from within me. My nakedness is strange to me already. My body seemed outdated. As if I were some foreign species, not fit for any human to see. I felt like waste. The frown on my face, coupled with shock was extremely visible as I tried to get into the shower. When was the last time I had used this? The showerhead was rusted, hadn't been replaced since I was 6, so I am surprised it has held on for that long. Cold water exploded in my face unexpectedly as I frantically tried to get the shower to work with me. With my fingers slipping through the reflective porcelain of the shower faucets. Eventually it did work with me, and so began my journey to cleanliness. My hair immediately presented itself in front of my face the second a droplet of water hit, stretching itself beyond my nose. It blocked my vision as I began my attempt at cleaning myself by continually rubbing my pathetic mop on the top of my head.

Seeing the pores, the dirt accumulated in one space, felt satisfying to scrub it away, ridding my body of these impurities I had engulfed by not showering. After what had happened yesterday, the shower felt like a natural progression, in order to digest the events properly.

I grabbed the same Old Spice shampoo my father used and applied it. Granted, I didn't know how to, I just applied it out of pure instinct. Going in between the flabs of my body and the folds of my skin. It smelled, odd. Like some sort of mint. I took a deep breath and turned off the shower. I shook my head, seeing the pockets of mould in between the corners of the shower, with water droplets splattering all along those pockets. I ripped the curtain, and I was back into that valley of steam. Smelling that mint scented shampoo that I had just let invade my entire body. It had been a while since I had taken such a shower, such a cleansing ritual due to my lack of self-worth and respect for myself.

I looked at my body once more. The folds in between my skin, the fat ruthlessly staring me in the face. I really was undesirable. I really was ugly. I grabbed the towel and quickly dried myself and put the fresh set of clothes on.

What was I going to do for the rest of the day? I went on my phone and booked a train ticket back to the city. It departed at 8.

I felt my eyes roll back; they were sticky. I had been awake so long last night, the light was dimmed and the only thing I could see was the glare of the computer screen. During the hours I spent scrolling, I educated myself on the hopelessness of our type of people when it comes to dating and women. I felt comforted, but the memories came back to me, ones that I didn't want to remember. Ones that I questioned. Why had I been so hopeless with women? I was rambling too much. It was almost time for me to see Remi again. The same man I dragged to a motel last night.

I opened one of the bags that I failed to unpack earlier, and grabbed my old, ripped up leather jacket. It had withstood a fair amount to get to this point, I had been wearing it most days it was too cold to get to a lecture. The white stripes along the top had faded, and the leather had also started to wear. I wore it, and immediately got the scent of that leather. I turned on the light and shortly realised the time I had spent messing about. I stood there for a couple seconds; my mind drew to a sharp standstill. I couldn't think, I felt just for those seconds, that I was in a trance of some sort, unable to articulate what I was feeling. I can't say I wasn't disturbed. I didn't know why I turned on the light, because I was about to leave. I walked through the living room. My mother was knitting. Just as she had done for most of my childhood.

The sounds of knitting always pissed me off, but I felt a sense of home whenever I would hear it anywhere.

"Where are you going? And you haven't left your room in 3 hours" my mother said, dropping her knitting gear. She seemed angry, mainly because I hadn't left that room. But I always hid in my room. Especially when I was living with my parents.

"Oh, I'm looking for a job".

I said, as I scanned for any snacks I could take. I eventually settled on another bag of Cheetos. It was the only thing available, but i was not complaining.

My mother nodded and allowed me to leave. Once again, it was not like she had any control over me anymore. She just carried on her knitting. However, she did look concerned. Who knows what I would do? I was not to be trusted. Even I knew that.

I checked my phone once more as I left the house. I took a good look at the sky. It was the time of day where the sky would look hazy, it was some sort of orange in tone. And for once, the neighbour and her son weren't having an argument. The station was only a 2-minute walk away. I checked my phone again. 7:45PM. I put my hands in the pockets of the leather jacket, I was starting to regret it now, the heat had really set in by the time I almost reached the station. In all honesty, I did not want to board a train again. After what had happened with that guy, who knows what I was going to witness next.

I hopped onto the train, and as I did, I got a text from Remi.

"Are you on your way?"

I replied with 'yes' and put my phone away. Why was I even doing this? I could have stayed home and done fuck all, but now I was heading to meet with Remi, having no idea about what he was going to say, or even do. Leaving Oakland, a day after I had arrived. I had no purpose anyways. Yet still, I had no idea what I was needed for. I had an odd sensation as the train moved. Almost as if what I was doing was dangerous.

Luckily, there were no absurd occurrences whilst I was on this train. I got off, right outside where we were supposed to meet, and put back on my dark leather jacket. It was not as hot right now; I had been in that train for so long that I didn't realise the change in temperature. The 'club' that Remi had mentioned was a well-known strip club; one I hadn't been to before, nor have any intention of going to anytime soon. We were meeting outside anyhow; I didn't want to cast eyes on any woman in my peripheral. I've already got the notion of disgust stored in my head every time I lay eyes on one. Once you have little to no attention from the opposite sex for a prolonged period, you best understand that you are a threat to them, or worse, a 'pervert' which I have had the dishonour of being called, multiple times.

As I approached the club, I heard men chanting for 'dances' from women, and nasty silhouettes of women on top of men's laps also cast themselves into my view. I always believed in the fallacy of 'true love' but hearing the commotion around this club, I refuse to believe in it anymore. Some of these men ought to be married. Yet even the oldest of men were enjoying the company of women who had no dignity, dancing all over their 5 inch dicks. I could only see from the outside though; I wouldn't dare walk in. Besides it was a place I was all too familiar with. My roommate, Sal used to frequently bring girls back to his dorm directly from this place. I knew this because they would demand payment whilst in his room and usually, he would not be able to pay them. That usually caused a fight, but he knew just where to find the 'right' ones, (a.k.a ones who were new to the industry who would never come back after he refused to pay.) But here I am. At this venue of deviance. As I was in awe of this place I sense a tap on my shoulder.

THE WORLD'S REVENGE

REMI PALLUDAN, 11ᵀᴴ JUNE 2013

I open the door of my shitty apartment I had rented for a couple months, I get inside my room I had been festering in for 30 years. The smell of sweat, old Chinese food and shit never fades away even if you drown the room with aerosols. Posters from 10 years prior looked faded as they were stuck up in the corner, with the only thing being new, my laptop upon my desk riddled with even more shit.

I put down my things from yet another nightmare shift and sat down at the desk where I would enact the greatest acts of heresy against society. I had a plan, a plan that would transcend the greatest acts done by one intending for societal change in a while. Women. How I hated those wretched beings. They were everything that was wrong with this world, the pain could not be imagined or conceived to me, and they bore the greatest burden to society. My life was a tragedy, that not even the likes of Shakespeare could write. And the only thing that was to be credited for it was women. The female gender. This pure-bred hatred was a catalyst for me to keep on feverishly writing, writing until my hands went sore, writing so that every woman on this earth would succumb to the metaphoric wound inflicted by it, and writing so my pains could slowly be erased, like the comfort of alcohol.

What did I write you may ask? It is a manifesto, a doctrine of purity amongst the sharp tides of hatred I so desperately wanted to inflict upon any woman in sight. I would look ominously for ideas, and as would do, I encountered the sight of an old photo, one from ten years prior. Even I could be shocked sometimes. My life only took this turn in the summer, the fateful summer of 2009. 23 years of age, the age in which most people start to get a companion which would be to the expense of every other man there. It was all a competition amongst the men. To see who had the most ability amongst us to ascertain the inevitable reward of female attention.

I for one, was strongly met with distain from any woman in sight, my attributes paled in comparison to some of the other so called 'masculine males' out there.

The summer was an opportunity, a chance, a last-ditch effort to garner attention from women. Where I could lose my curse that they called 'virginity'. The opportunity arose nevertheless, and I intended to take it. The graduation party, the very essence of it drew my sullen confidence up. My head swells up with regret every time my conscience brings me to direct thought to it, as I try to forget the events that so callously transpired that day.

I decided that the predominant reason as to why I could not get any female in sight was attributed to the fact that I had no confidence, and for this 'party', I intended to rectify that. How nonsensical that decision was. I made the fateful decision to venture out of my comfort zone and attend that degenerate coup.

I had the naive conception that I may have been able to appear conventionally 'attractive' to at least one of these wretches, but upon arrival, it was very clear to my mind, they would not be in my favour. I try not to remember it much, but for the sake of my account I will attempt to reconstruct.

We had just graduated. I, like many others of my age group decided to attend the graduation afterparty in order to hopefully and finally get females. The afternoon was spent rummaging through my wardrobe looking for something to wear, eventually settling on a suit jacket and a smart shirt with a tie. I finished off with applying a hefty amount of hair gel to my hair, and styling it, just how I had seen those high value men, the pricks who had somehow been classed as 'popular' and 'high value' amongst the race of men did. For once, I felt some false sense of confidence in my appearance and knew that women would gravitate towards it. That day, my dense brain assumed that I would be able to find some sort of companionship, despite being the one classed as 'weird' for most of my life. That day was meant to be one of change and realisation. But what the harsh and bitter reality was I would get unimaginable levels of hate for anything to do with women from that day forward.

I had always been conditioned to believe that I was meant to be 'nice' to these heartless scumbags, yet that day and days that preceded it gave me a harsh reminder of who I really was. An emotional, washed up 'gentleman' who could not gain any forms of female attention, and would not go on to live a decent and fulfilling life. Scouring for my purpose amongst a sea of men who compete for differing levels of value, admiration and validity from these 'women'. God. I have deviated too much. I must go back to the narrative.

I had later arrived in my parents' car to the separate venue where the graduation party would take place, and upon arrival, I caught sight of the woman I had fantasised about continuously for the past three years, Meredith. She wore a tight black dress, her eyes were bold and black, her skin was clear and free of any blemishes and her luscious hair flowed in directions I had never seen before, her beauty was to be worshipped, and it was, by me.

I tried fixing up my hair as I walked toward the venue and analysed the surrounding area. Exactly what I had expected. I felt a torrent of sexual energy emerge from the depths of my soul and looking at all those women helped me ponder further, which ones I would go out with. But my mind remained fixated on that one celestial, charming female Meredith, in the corner of the room. She was not like the other 'whores' in the same area, she carried with herself, an aura of femininity. Something that was lost cause in the society at large. I held my hopes that she had fidelity – and would remain committed to me for the rest of time, and that day, I envisioned myself going out with her and subsequently spending my entire future with her. When I filled with that aspect of desperation, my mind wanted, and needed to approach her. I had never touched a woman before, and now to me that was something forbidden, yet I still carried curiosity whenever I would attempt to touch them.

I spent a good hour at the party, pacing around, hoping that today would finally be the day my sorrow fortunes would change.

It led to the single worst experience my life has ever been involved in. The event that ruined me. The dancing.

Everyone was immersed in celebration, including Meredith. I had decided that I could at least attempt to touch her, and see how she feels, the sweet female touch that my body longed for uncontrollably. I did not know how to dance, I attempted to 'blend in', but that was a painful experience. I trudged through to find her amongst the immense crowds of people, and there she was. With me tightly packed between the hordes of people dancing to late 2000s hip hop, it amplified my opportunity. I looked at my hand before I attempted to feel the soft enigmatic touch, and went in. My hand sunk in closer and closer until it met the soft, luscious fabric. Once I felt it, I could never let go. It was positioned at the perfect curve so I could feel her hips swaying from side to side and closed my eyes to fully immerse myself in her. I had done it, a woman had been touched, a beautiful one at that. Everything had just come full circle. But amongst the hypnosis her body gave me, the contrast of the soft fabric touch was equally met with a large thud, a burst of pain and irritation on my jaw, marks brandished upon my face, as a scream could be heard amongst all of it. My memory was blurry, but the only thing I could feel was the feeling of my face dropping to the ground, and gasps erupting from the people dancing.

"You fucking pervert, beat him up" were the words that I could hear amongst the concussion I had just sustained. I felt multiple harrowing thuds rain down upon me, the pain unimaginable, as I covered my face. I open my eyes, staring quickly in shock of what had just happened, for just a second and as I did, I encountered a man, brown skin, with a six-foot nine stature. He towered over my shrivelled body and directed two other guys to stop raining hell on me. He must have been from Samoa, or somewhere around there as he had a thick Australian accent, with exotic looking eyes. Deep black tribal tattoos emblazoned on his brown body.

"Call the police on this fucking pervert."

He looked at me, charged with strong rage. I had fear hidden deep within me as I rushed to look for Meredith. She disappeared almost. I quickly scanned to find her, yet nothing was uncovered. Still, her space had been violated. What had I done?

"How dare you touch my girlfriend like that you disgusting shithead" he said whilst maintaining his sharp glance toward me. "Touch her again and I'll fucking kill you". He then proceeded to kick me as he went to comfort her. Of course, to tame his masculinity. I knew that no one would ever go out with me, and this ruined my chances completely. But of course, a woman who carried with her that level of beauty was bound to have a companion ten times as masculine as me.

I got yanked up and got escorted out of the venue with wounds all over me, and people heckling me from the inside.

My chances were ruined to ever find a woman. My head was still spinning, as I, without purpose or strength, attempted to walk away from the scene and never step foot in that college again.

From that day forward, it changed my fortunes. As I returned home, I vowed to never see any woman again. It was upon that day I came to an epiphany – to declare war against the female species and stop any self-respecting male to even think about 'dating'. It was all an illusion. A ploy to trap males into a system of exploitation. In that moment, I started to go on a psychotic rampage, the likes of which no one had ever seen before.

I ran my fingers through my hair and rummaged it. I needed to go back to my bedraggled, worthless state. I could not bear witness any more of my antics trying to get women. All for fucking nothing. I began wailing, hoping somebody would feel some sympathy for me, but no one did listen. In that moment, I knew what my destiny would be. And I will embrace that destiny and vow to spark retribution upon members of the female gender.

I am Remi Palludan, and I shall destroy the female race.

STACY

I felt a tap on my shoulder. It was Remi. He glanced at me and pulled me aside.

The back of this nightclub. I could hear the drowned-out noise of what everybody was doing as Remi opened a bag he had brought. My heartbeat multiplied as I braced myself for whatever was going to occur once he reached in there. But no. He pulled out a wad of bills and handed them to me, with a polaroid photo also in his hands. The polaroid was of a woman, with beautiful brunette hair, and a face that was extremely appealing. Even to myself.
"There's 200 in that stack" he said.

"Remi... I can't take this" I said back, whilst handing back the stack of cash.
"It's the least I can give you after you helped me out last night" he said, as he looked awkwardly in my direction. "You were good company aswell"
"Well, thanks I really appreciate it. Are you sure you want to give this to me?" after all, I'd only known him for a night, how could he give me so much money?
"Just don't second guess it, take it goddamnit" as he placed them in my hand forcefully.
"Who's the girl, if you don't mind me asking?" I said. The polaroid image surely did her beauty justice.
"It's that fucking whore, Meredith. I thought you should have it to see what a fucking slut looks like" he said, as his facial expression changed drastically. So that was 'Meredith'. The same woman he had heckled after he was kicked out of the bar.
I felt cagey on entrusting Remi, but my mind kept assuming I had gone too deep in to pull out now. I pocketed the money, small

enough to fit there, and thanked Remi again as I made my way for the station. I was confused as to why he would give me that amount of money for a simple task. I wasn't complaining, neither would anyone in my exact position. I took a glance at this club for one last time, I saw men with stubble like beards smoking cigarettes at the front depleted of any purpose or cause in life. I travelled an hour for a stack of dollar bills. It had to be something important – yet I had the belief that Remi was plotting something bigger, the amount of suffering I have faced as a result of my appearance could
not be understated. I vowed to Remi, that I would stick by his side, no matter what. For opening my sullen eyes, for helping me to understand why I cannot and will not ever, find a companion.
He looks at the ground, and then turns back to me, and says:
"Let's meet at the shooting range next week. I'll show you something".

I had never received an invite like this before, to play around with guns and extract my revenge in a method that had not been seen previously. I agreed and attempted to get back home.

LOST

RICARDO JOAQUIN CASTILLO, 14TH JUNE 2013

I was about to make my way to yet another endeavour with Remi, yet this time, I was excited about it. It had been a week, most of that time was spent doing mundane things whilst in solitude.

As I approached the door, my 'father' also walks to do the same. He stops me and looks at me. As he did, waves of unwanted, distorted nostalgia planted itself in my mind.

"When are you getting a job you lazy sack of shit"

My mind, which had just previously been chugging with emotions, thoughts and ruminations, had stopped. Everything stopped in my mind. It was as if time had stopped itself. Was this a torrent of rage? I could only see red, I could only see the situation I had found myself in getting worse, thanks to my 'father'.

"Last time I checked you weren't my real father. You can't give me instructions"

How dare he insult me like this. I had only been in the house for a few short days, yet he feels as if I were a burden. His feelings have no bearings on me. His moustache, white with specks of black on it, moved up. It was almost as if he was going to let out some laughter. This was no laughing matter.

"You're in my house, you fucking failure. You abide by my rules here. Now your sorry ass is lucky I am not your father, I would have whipped you in to shape long before." He had crossed the line in every conceivable way. His presence was simply infuriating to me, I I needed to do something, I needed to retaliate.

"Now you get a job, or at least try to get a job before things turn ugly in this household."

And with that, he slammed the door shut. Fuck I hated him, to the point I would sometimes wish death upon him. It was justified. This was the same guy who couldn't provide for our family, refusing to work. I was immensely surprised he was the one arguing.

My mother looked on as I stood there, with shivers raining down across me. I was a failure. He was right. I could not retaliate. Despite him not being a father to me, what he said in that moment, reflected everything I had envisioned in my mind. I just needed someone to explicitly say it to me. Say what needed to be said.

I waited for a while until I left, without saying a word, it was merely reflective and filled with self-hatred. I felt, lost. Everything I was dreading was now coming to fruition.

I attempted to take my mind off it, by eventually visiting this shooting range with Remi. I had entered, and upon entry, was greeted by a man, large beard, with a ripped-up orange cap. I gave him a 20-dollar bill from the stack of cash I was lugging around on my person, and he directed me to one of the stations.

"You ready to let all that rage out?"

He looked at me with a gleam in his eye. One I had never seen before in the few days of knowing him. He grabbed the assault rifle that was perched up in this cubicle that we shared, and shot at a paper looking man, with holes piercing his stomach with every shot.

 "It seems like you've used one of these things before" I said, whilst he took off those sound cancelling earphones.

"Ricardo, I own multiple shotguns, I'm an expert at these motherfuckers"

He did this whilst proudly handing the rifle to me. This was it. My first time utilising a weapon. It was a rather peculiar sight. Holding this felt like I had all the power in the world. A sense of power over those pricks who would pin me against lockers, a sense of power over the girl who heckled me on the train, a sense of power over that prick who assaulted that same girl. It was enigmatic to me in some twisted way.

"Are you going to shoot it, or just stand there like an idiot"

Remi peered over my shoulder. I adjusted the grip and looked onward to that paper man. Fresh off a fight with my 'father', I had fresh, ripe rage stored up inside of me, ready to be excreted by shooting. Firing multiple rounds of bullets, that pierced the paper of the target. I began seeing my father in that one moment, with all that rage stored in me from the ordeal we had just solicited, and I could not help but envision him in those bullets. My gun technique was shaky – I couldn't hold it properly, but it felt liberating in that moment, to handle something as exciting as a firearm, despite the shots all going wayward. I didn't hit a single target in that barrage. Remi glanced, shocked as he saw me handle that weapon with finesse.

"Have you shot a gun before?"

"No. This is the first time I'm using one"

He looked, perplexed that this was the first time I had discovered the pleasure of the 'gun'.

"You handled that very well, I wouldn't have known this was your first time using one". He said, clearing up the shooting rack.

I felt flattered, as I put the gun down. It was a sense of liberation and pride. I took off those muffle headphones for a brief second and watched on as Remi piled on heaps of rage through the rounds of bullets he shot.

"Now imagine Meredith is there"

I laughed as he kept piling on the heat, but something told me he was being serious beyond the joke he had just made.

Who was Meredith?

THE WORLD'S REVENGE

REMI PALLUDAN, 14 JUNE 2009

Vengeance. It was the only thing I would think about in that moment, the only thing keeping me alive at that point. It felt like purgatory, seeing all these criminals in one room, together. What crime they had committed had no meaning to me. I could not look myself in the eye at that moment, let alone think about other people. I sat, slouched on this cheap plastic chair, waiting for my inevitable punishment as I clenched my hand in to a fist. The same fist I had seen that 6'9 Samoan make as he was raining hell all over me. Going to that party was the worst decision I made, as I waited for my fate in this police waiting room. How I held Meredith on a pedestal all these years, only for her to destroy every essence of my being in a matter of minutes. It made me hate women even more.

My life had been destroyed for everyone to see. It enraged me to the point of no return, the way I was heckled, the public arrest, it would be justified to end my sad life right here and now.

"Remi Palludan?"

Looks like I'm up. I walked with this female officer, into a cold room with what looked to be a detective.

"Take a seat, Palludan"

I followed suit and sat down. I took this opportunity to look around the room, observed this place properly.

"Alright, so according to a couple witnesses, you have apparently been caught groping a woman at a graduation party, is this correct?"

He looked at me, with a sheepish look in his eye. He knew I had been detained at the venue, why ask?

"Yes I did".

"And you got assaulted by a group of men for this, is that correct?"

"Yes". I answered, as I rubbed the bruise above my eye.

I could not go to jail. My retribution had not even begun yet, I had so much hate it was unfathomable to ordinary human minds. There was no use just rotting in a jail cell, my life had so much more to offer. The officer began writing up some form of document and sighed as he explained stoically – "Well, Remi since you haven't committed any prior offences, we are going to let you go, but we've issued a restraining order for you upon the request of Meredith Catherine Brown, and we are going to need to add you to the sex offender's registry, this may limit you from getting a job, or other endeavours, do you understand?"

Great. However, the only thing I thought about in that moment was the fact that they would let me go free. Nothing else.

"I understand"

Truth be told, the rest of the narrative was signing documents and declarations, but my retribution had not arisen yet. I could not forgive anyone for the injustices that had been dealt to me, and I for one, could not simply stand around and wait for the tragedy to occur, rather I would combat this tragedy with my retribution against the female gender. Meredith was everything I wanted, everything I needed in order to not spark this period, but she turned on me. Just like the hundreds that did.

The next couple of days were spent in relative solitude, in my room, those days turned into weeks, those weeks into months. All were spent, away in my room, away from society. The fear I had of people, specifically women - had multiplied as a result of this. And now, I was a new addition to the sex offender's registry. Festering in a room was not ideal, even I knew this. This prompted me to fall into a deep spiral of depression. A state I could not escape out of, a state of self-hatred and loathing. What could I do to mitigate these sorrow, sullen feelings? At that point I could physically feel the pressures of life weighing down upon me, the responsibilities I had to bear now in my so called 'maturity', were becoming more of a burden every day I lived. I would try and escape these feelings through going on long walks in parks, and attempting to keep a tight schedule, a 'routine' if you will, and forcing myself to get away from all of it. Yet still, these feelings did not escape easily. In fact, at certain times, going on walks was the worst activity I could have done. The sights of emotionally stable men, those who looked like they kept a vigorous routine, and took care of themselves physically would spur me into deep jealousies, the likes of which I could not escape out of for days on end. The worst sight of all, however, was men who seemed to possess a complete and happy family, with a wife and children. At the time, it would grind me to the core, but now at the age of 30, it makes my essence feel minuscule, insignificant and draws me to hatred upon the sight of these men who have accomplished some good fortune in their lives. At the time, I would sit down on the park benches, and question – *Why was I like this?* And, truth be told, I had the hapless realisation that my life was soon going to be anything but ideal. I felt a sense of worthlessness next to these types of men, ones who had a sense of direction in their lives, ones who had the mental stability to produce offspring, and pass on life lessons that they had learnt to their children. This power that I could not achieve was eating me up from the inside, constantly thinking how I could gain some form of upper hand against these men who I perceived as a threat. I could not stand another minute on this earth without having any power. I needed dominance, something that could lift me above all those other men. My walks, for the most part, continued as normal, despite my desperation for dominance, and I attempted to avoid accomplished looking men. Even now at 30, I cannot bear the sight, knowing that a man is above you in every conceivable way does irreversible damage to one's mental state and shatters you in ways that you cannot imagine. I was consumed by jealousy yet hated women with every ounce of my being, seeing those men made me even more desperate for power over them, all the happiness had been stolen and sucked out of me, yet these men were thriving and living happy lives? I didn't want to call myself a failure just yet, but from what was happening around me every single time I would step outside, it certainly seemed as if it was heading that way.

I could not let that happen. I needed power, I needed something that could give me strength over all those who I encounter daily, and it was with that, I settled on immediately attaining a gun licence and gaining power through owning a firearm. After hours of research, scouring through the internet, combing through forums, I settled on the simple, compact semi-automatic pistol. It provided everything I needed for one like myself to feel a sense of dominance. I swore to myself however, that I would seldom utilise it. It would simply be a last resort. Even amongst all the injustices that the world had caused me, I still did not have the mental capacity to open fire on people and commit the deed of killings. However, I still have not achieved the levels of excitement I had when I received my gun licence. One of the lights that shone during what was, an immensely dark period in my life at that point. Immediately, I set foot towards a gun store near to my residence, I knew it well, from all those days at college I would pass it and catch glimpse of middle-aged men practicing with semi-automatic rifles and pistols. It felt surreal going inside of what had been an enigma for years. And I felt emotions I could not even describe upon entering. Amongst the array of different guns scattered across the shop floor, I could see the exact weapon I had been fantasising about. The semi-automatic pistol. It was calling out towards me, and I intended to fulfil that call by purchasing it.

I had never shot a gun, which was something I intended to pursue upon buying the firearm. And once I did, it was exactly how I had envisioned it in my twisted mind. The bullets leaving the barrel left me with the strongest feelings of gleam and fulfilment that I have seldom, experienced before. I felt my worth as a man, shooting at a target with great accuracy and might. I could not wait any longer to purchase it. I needed this sense of power in my life. I had a small amount of money saved up, and I utilised it all on this powerful object. The tingles still radiate through my body the second it had entered my grasp. It was as if it were an amulet, hidden in the depths of Egypt, created for the sole discovery, by me. I felt power over that Samoan who beat me to a pulp, I felt power over Meredith, I felt power over all those who swore to oppress me, I felt all those people below a being like myself. This gun has given me new life from the second I began using it. But this very instrument only fuelled what was a tormented mental state, for me at least.

I had been released from my shackles. I did not intend to kill, but now nothing could hold me back. Nothing could arise from the shadows and defeat me, for I could rebel against every being with just a singular shot from this gun.

With the acquisition of this firearm, began the start of my downward spiral. What was a hatred for women turned into a deep and dangerous loathing and melancholy. Seeing women with men had always been a difficult and hard sight, but now with this gun tucked away in the shadows, I felt like opening fire on every single couple I would lay eyes upon. I only had one whore to blame. Meredith Catherine Brown. That beating I had received would play frequently in my nightmares, the sheer horror I experienced upon envisioning that Samoan, towering over my dishevelled, curled up body, those horrors, could not be replicated again. I would not let it happen. Yet, every night it tormented me. Her name, the mere recollection of it drove me into an even deeper depressive state, made worse by my vivid memory of the touch I felt that night, her perfect body was something I still admired despite being torn to shreds by a bestial being.

And it is with this, I must stress, the power of the human mind. What torment that I went through as a result of it. I needed solace, guidance, and a way to express my deep sorrows and retribution to the world. To end this seemingly endless vein of suffering and pain I would wake up to daily.

In this depressive state, I became chronically engrossed online. I joined communities to try and divert my shaken mind away from my life being effectively ruined. The nightmares persisted, making my life a living sense of guilt, regret and resentment. It did not help that my parents were on me, trying to force me into employment. I dreaded every waking second, every time I had to see my parents, in fear that they would berate me with questions and insults. I knew I was not in the correct mental state to be alive, let alone working. My walks continued, with twisted thoughts coming to mind every single time I would see anyone who had a happy life. If anything, the gun made me worse, as I would continue to think of ways to kill those people walking past, my mind becoming at war with words inside my twisted, dark head.

Parents would hide their children from me as I would waddle past, citing me as some sort of monster, someone to be feared. The men would look at me, giving themselves a boost with their own self-image upon staring at my hideous stature, and worst of all were the women, who would feel sexually assaulted every time they laid eyes on me. My life quickly spiralled into disaster, with my name on the sex offender's registry, fresh off a beating from a Samoan, and my confidence at an all-time low, it only will fuel my rebuttal against the female gender. Despite these immoral thoughts against women, I still possessed a sex drive. Just as any other man would. Denying it would be a lie, but it was something I now knew I could never attain. I was a sex offender now, the world was now against me, and I now had to navigate this sullen land myself, with no help.

My parents later suggested I went to therapy, as a result of my concerning and deteriorating mental state. Coupled with high levels of insomnia, they had all the reason to be worried for what I was slowly becoming.

I couldn't bear the thought of expressing my true desires and feelings to another human. They would surely bring about the end of my life as a free man. As much as I knew my mental state was immensely flawed, if I wanted to gain my revenge, I simply could not reveal my condition to a therapist. I declined repeatedly, and so carried on with my degenerate life.

I knew deep down that therapy may have been beneficial for my life, but I could not agree. I had believed I was a powerful being. One who could not succumb to being weakened by speaking about my feelings. I had also somehow managed to hide the gun from my parents, it would only make them question my mental state further, seeing a weapon stashed in my room. I had now discovered a new forum, one where nothing was off limits, where you could express the wildest desires and flaws you had, and this was perfect for my torment. It was this exact place; I was exposed to the horrors and subsequent pleasure of gore. The idea of watching another human in distress and pain, with their face in disarray, their stifled screams and desperation in their voice, provided me with an odd sense of satisfaction. In the disastrous manner my life was headed, it provided a much-needed gratitude for my own conscience. It didn't bear long until I was desensitized to the nature of death, seeing endless amounts of beheadings and killings, left me with sanctity each time I would see it. It didn't stop the insanity, however. My nightmares carried on for months, those months spent without the solace of productivity.

Every nightmare was something different, but in every single one of these, I saw the Samoan. That six-foot nine beast would torment me for months on end. It had been months since that party, and the image of him towering above my body could not escape my mind. That kick, his enigmatic Australian accent, his protectiveness over Meredith, it all tormented me. It was a dark cloud over my life, something I could not move on from.

Spending my time on walks, around nature had taken its toll, nature had now become a curse without a companion to appreciate it with. Humans need companions. Without it, we are incomplete. That was one of the things I had learned from constantly having the curse of viewing successful couples. I continue to question, at the age of 30, what it would be like with a woman, someone who cares for me, loves me romantically, and sees past my obvious flaws. Now I see past that. My youth is over. The opportunity for a successful life was now over. The only thing left, is my revenge. My life however, was far from over. A new beginning had emerged.

LAPSE

RICARDO JOAQUIN CASTILLO

It had been 2 months since I had been introduced into Remi's world. This world was something foreign; alluring to someone like me, and I sought refuge from it. I tried to seize contact with Remi, yet I still hung around in his presence. I could feel my life spiralling out of control by following his actions every waking second. Actions, which often involved violence. Our constant visits to strip clubs, and bars made me feel anything but fulfilment. It only made me sulk into even more depression.

It felt like years since I had attended my graduation, my diploma was framed above my desk of degeneracy like some sort of trinket. That's all it was for now. It didn't hold any purpose. If I did eventually get a job, I would hold a great deal of sorrow every single day. Getting up at 8am sharp, living off cheap coffee, coming home to most likely a wife who doesn't respect me, a child who is spoiled shitless and lukewarm food served on cheap plastic plates. I may be reaching far, but this was the direction I sought as the most likely eventuality for my life. I knew Remi way better now, after visiting many clubs with him. He no longer seemed 'alien' to me. After all, as much as I lament the lifestyle he leads, it seems I myself, will veer towards that outcome. The neighbourhood we lived in didn't seem too keen of 'people' like us. Who wouldn't be?

Every single passing day would come and go quick. I felt the pressure of growing up as I sat there, wallowing in a seat for ten hours a day, doing nothing but endless scouring on the internet and heavy drinking, and I had no doubt Remi would do the same.

My rift with my parents soon worsened, and it was only a matter of time before my father would do something about my freeloading and club visits. I had some money saved, around $1000 to make sure that I wouldn't be stranded if worse got too worse.

In this time, I would spend in self-pity and doubt, I began entering the online lottery. At the time it felt alluring, however now all those times spent entering and losing took its toll. To me, it felt like the only way I could escape my troubles at home. On very rare occasions, I would come to the harrowing conclusion that my life may end up like Remi's. As much as I would speak of the respect I had for him, I knew that a life like his would only lead to more depression. He was the only person I would speak to, despite my efforts to try and distance myself. But it was hard, when you can relate to someone and their life experiences but still want to break out of a relentless cycle. I was very much still in this world that I had been exposed to. Was I trapped?

I had no idea that today would be the last straw for my existence in my parents' household. I had started the day as normal, waddling to the kitchen to fulfil my hunger quota, sitting around the house doing anything but productivity, and checking the online lottery numbers. A couple hours had passed since I had awoken, and I was sat there, on my so-called desk of degeneracy. I overheard my parents, bickering and arguing through the thin wooden walls. I sought to ignore it, carrying on with my mundane tasks. The noises from the room became louder, and I braced myself for a potential brawl between them. I never stopped to listen to what they argued about, which later became abhorrently clear when my 'father' aggressively banged on my bedroom door.

The reflection on my computer screen displayed my eyes widening, clenching my hand into a fist, as I would always do when feeling threatened. The banging became louder with my mother aggressively saying 'Stop' in Spanish. I stopped for a second and took a hard breath and shut my eyes for one singular second. I arose from my chair, making a creaking sound as my backside levitated away from it, and I opened the door. Immediately as I did, my father pushed up against my face and pushed my frail fat body.

"How long is your ass going to keep freeloading?"
He had a serious, determined look written all over his face when he said it. I for one, was still in shock for him pushing me. My mother, screaming over his broken words.
"You fucking fatass, we actually thought you would get a job and stop being a lazy sack of shit, fucking about every single day in strip clubs. How about you get married?"
He threw a whole dictionary of insults towards me, and I stood there, attempting to look unfazed as I stared the $1000 in the face.
I couldn't string a sentence together against him.
It was as if the whole world had become a blur in front of my very eyes. This wasn't my real father, yet here he is berating my entire existence.
"Listen you fucking failure. You have ten hours to get the hell out of my house, or I'm calling the cops. I don't give a fuck where you go, I want you out. Is that clear?"

My mother stood there in shock, and in silence. She was powerless against him. It was his house above all else. I would proceed to nod in agreement as he repeats – "10 hours".

It looks like my time in my parents' house had come to an end. Immediately, I took the $1000 I had and counted it once more. I made sure that I had enough. Amongst this, my innocent mother was victim to his horrendous voice standing by his decision to oust me from the house. I needed to agree with it, as neither I nor my mother had any power against him.

Who could blame my father for his actions? I had argued with him in the past but now I had no choice but to go along with his decision. I did in fact need to leave as soon as humanly possible. My parents were still violently arguing in the background, but I dismissed it now in order to prepare for what I needed to do once I was forced to leave.

I began compiling my things, the first thing being my computer, as well as all the accessories that came with it, back in that familiar spot in my suitcase. The multiple jackets I owned as well as the diploma I also then stuffed inside. My shirts were crumpled to the highest extent, after too many instances of neglecting the washing. I kept them in that state as I would put them into the suitcase and closed it. The whole process took an hour at most, all the while the bickering my parents were engaged in not calming down in the slightest. It got louder now, every single time I would place an item inside the suitcase.

I sat down.

I took a seat on my bed, the place I have been festering in for the past few months.

I made the impulsive decision to open my suitcase once more and grab the diploma I had stuffed within it. It had no meaning or purpose to me anymore. I had no ambitions of getting a job at this point. Would it even have a purpose once I leave these four walls? How much does a diploma mean now that I have become effectively homeless? How much did it mean to that fucker Remi? Spending his life slaving away at a supermarket, now spending his life gambling, and getting with prostitutes every single night. The man is 30 years of age. My hands began to tremble, tremors ran through the veins of them. I paid little attention to the fine print inscribed on the gold paper. That's all it was. A piece of paper. A piece of minuscule, insignificant paper. What lied behind the enchantment of the word 'diploma', to people like myself was a life of pain, devastation, getting up every day to pledge submission to someone you don't respect, getting married, having children who don't respect you, your wife moaning about your insignificant sexual performances, cheating on you because you have no time nor money for a gym membership to work on your frail, lacklustre body mainly due to the fact you have been slaving away all day to attain a 'standard of living' for your significant other that you cannot even do with the job you have. Maybe I am reaching, yet this was the reality I accepted up until this point.

I sat there.

Waiting.

I remained seated, my parents' voices began to drown out gradually. Still with this so called 'prestigious' document in my hands I arose from my bed. The small plastic trash can next to my desk would be the new home of this essence of false validation. I took one last glance at the gold letters inscribed upon the letter, and chucked it away. Just like that. 3 whole years of my life have vanished in one singular motion. What use would it have for me anyhow?

I grabbed my suitcase and opened the door. I took one last sight at my room for what could be the last time. I didn't feel an ounce of guilt. This was meant to be someplace I could call 'home'. One illegitimate 'father' had now squandered it.

I opened the door to reveal the living room. My frail mother sat there in that red recliner she would always retreat to and looked up. She had been crying relentlessly.

"Ricardo. Don't go."

"Please."

I touched her delicate chin with my hand. It felt, soothing. Her tears had soaked up onto her chin, making it soft to touch.

"I will come back. I'm only leaving for a few hours."

He face lit up once more. She stops for a moment to shoot a glance at my father's bedroom and gave me a look of reassurance.

I nodded at her. I could not spend any more time here, for my father would come out of his cigarette infested room and start engaging in a war of words with me.

I looked back once more as I left the room and saw her contagious smile. Who knew when I would return to it?

I left with no intention to return.

IGNORANT

RICARDO JOAQUIN CASTILLO

It would be there I stood, outside the suburban sprawl of the neighbourhood I once called 'home'. Suitcase in hand, I knew in that moment exactly who I would call. I scrambled in my pockets to reveal my phone, with its cracked screen on full display. I needed to contact Remi, as twisted as it would sound. I needed someplace to stay. I banked on the hope that he would provide shelter to me, despite the fact I refrained from speaking to him for weeks.

Who knew what he would think?

I braved the decision to call Remi, stood there for God knows how long staring at his contact information. I didn't feel as if he was ready to contact me. I needed to swallow whatever feelings I had conjured up, and make the call. In one impulsive second, I pressed on his contact information and called him. My fingers in a constant shiver as I would hold the phone to my ear. I felt it ring, and in that moment I had the overwhelming feeling of hanging up, finding a hostel someplace, but I had no time to hang up. As soon as I would hear the phone ring, I hear his voice, startling me for how quick it was.

"Remi?"

My voice had stuttered as I attempted to get the words out. I did try and distance myself after all.

"Ricardo. It's been a while, friend"

It was reassuring, hearing him address me as a 'friend', despite the fact he probably knew that I was trying my best to avoid him. Who could blame me? Even I knew a bad influence when I saw one. I took a deep breath that could be heard through the phone, and exclaimed, "It sure has been a while. How are things going with you?"

I eagerly waited for his response. For I had not asked the predominant reason I had called. He began to speak. "Same old bullshit week in, week out".

It didn't cease to surprise me his life had continued in mundane fashion. His life wasn't something to be proud of, either. In that moment, I could not exclaim what I wanted from him. Not over the phone, anyways. It felt weird to ask him there and then. I gave him a quick response, saying "Look man, why don't we meet at a Starbucks or something like that"

I immediately cringed as soon as those words left my mouth. It would feel out of character for Remi to visit a Starbucks. Those sorts of establishments are more in line for 17-year-old white chicks. I rushed to correct my statement.

"Maybe not a starbuck-"

"No. Let's meet there, if you are talking about the local one"

"Yeah, the local one. That one exactly. I'll see you there"

I let out a deep sigh upon ending the call. I started questioning myself, asking why I had not simply asked to crash at his home. Now I must meet him at a coffee place in which he would most likely interrogate me on what I had been doing for the past few months. Granted, he would have done the same if I had stayed at his house, but now I must speak to him, face to face. I have developed this new fear of Remi, one of endangerment whenever I would see him. Who knew what his intentions were? I looked up at the early moonlit sky, then looked back toward my former house, and carried the suitcase along the pavement. The wheels bouncing up and down as you would pull it, opposing the pebbles dotted along the path. I had no second thoughts about leaving my 'diploma' back at that house. Everything happened so suddenly I had no time to think. I knew my father would call the cops if I was ever seen there again, so I did lie to my mother. I would never return. I knew I needed to spend those $1000 in my grasp wisely. I was banking on the fact that Remi would allow me to live in his home and become an intruder. I asked him to meet me at the local 'Starbucks', and that's where I would be headed. To be with Remi in a public space is to carefully observe your surroundings and stay vigilant. To expect the stares and unsavoury attentive looks towards you, and not engage in any form of immoral discussions. I knew Remi enough to realise that he did not have any form of filter. He was a chronically online individual, and it showed whenever I would go to public spaces with him. The Starbucks was a short walk from where I lived, it took half an hour for my fat amalgamation of a body to reach.

Even for me, visiting a place like Starbucks was out of character. Yet it was the only place that slipped out of my mouth at the time. I could ask no questions; it would only make my encounter a tougher experience.

It didn't help for when I entered the Starbucks, that I had a huge suitcase packed with items. That was made even more prevalent when I entered. Filled to the brim with people with the body weight of skeletons, a far cry from what I was. My social anxiety shot up tenfold, as I scanned around the place looking for Remi. My eyes shot at all angles at a faster pace, I felt the weight of those wretches' eyes around me scanning every inch of my body, the folds, the sweat droplets I could feel running down every inch of my forehead, the giant suitcase which created a major inconvenience for all that bore witness. In that moment, I needed to depart immediately. Luckily, I managed to find a seat and I waddled toward it with haste. I could finally relieve that pain swelling inside my legs, and blend in the best I could with the rest of the skeletons inside this establishment. My legs were spread across the entire length of the seat, taking up every single inch with my lacklustre excuse of a body.

It wasn't long until I saw Remi also waddle inside the place. I could tell him apart from every single person in there. He shared the same fat, flab filled build after all. His hair, unwashed and greasy, it looked like he just rolled out of bed. His eyes were a good indicator of this.

I cringed when I saw the amount of people staring at him with faces of disgust and woe. After all, neither Remi nor me fit in with the rest of these manufactured specimens.

He caught a glance of me and sat down on the opposite side of me.

"Ricardo" he said, with a rare smile irked upon his face.

"Not the place I would typically see you" he followed, slowly bending down to take a seat on the washed-out leather chair.

"I could say the same for you" I said, staring into his eyes with the blankness that emanated throughout my entire soul in the moment. By this point, he looked over my shoulder for a moment, and saw the suitcase I had stored vertically next to the leather seat I had inhabited.

"What's the suitcase for?"

I took a deep breath before I could speak my piece. It was more of a nerve-racking experience than I had initially conceived. If Remi would not let me stay at his place, it was too late to venture out to a hostel or motel. It also did not help that my phone was about to meet its demise soon. This was my one shot, or I would rot on the streets of Oakland, with other cracked out debauched individuals.

"Ricardo? What is that thing for?"

I clenched my hands into a fist as I always did.

"Well, the reason I asked you here is mainly because my parents decided to, uh kick me out of their house"

"I don't have anywhere to stay."

I hung my head in shame, not caring about the repercussions of what would happen if Remi had decided to go against letting me inside of his house.

Remi looked down, to align himself on my level, and squinted his eyes a small amount. Even he could understand the feeling of guilt, the feeling of dejection I was feeling in that very moment.

"You think I wouldn't let you stay in my house?"

I looked up, with a visible gleam from my eye, and widened my eyes a small amount.

Remi did not seem at all bothered I had been avoiding him for the past few months. He smiled as he opened his mouth again.

"Sure man, I mean I don't mind. It depends on my parents, but I'm cool with it"

I had a feeling of immense gratitude permeate throughout my body. I felt my bond become stronger with Remi in that moment, my whole world was turned upside down in a matter of minutes, I could not afford to sleep on the bleak, desolate streets.

"You want anything?" – he said as I took one last glance around the place. Nothing interested me. The chalkboard signage, the images of large glass mugs with whipped cream and sprinkles staring at you in the face, and sandwiches that were due to be reheated. For once in my tragic life, I did not have the appetite for food. Not in this shithole anyway.

"Nope. I think I'm alright"

Remi gave me a look of reassurance. Seems like he didn't want to waste any time here either.

"Well then, we ought to leave"

I took one last glance at the suitcase I had stored next to me and picked it up whilst also arising from my seat. The place was crowded, I made sure I checked my surroundings in case of any more unwanted encounters. We decided to make haste when leaving, and as we did, a group of what seemed like teenagers barged in front of me. Just the type you would see scouring in shopping malls, the ones the girls would mindlessly throw themselves towards, and show no respect for their fathers in doing so. I quickly apologised and saw the light in the exit. As I tried to distance myself from the situation, I could hear a distant address towards me.

"Hey fatass, watch yourself".

I could tell it came from one of those boys in the group. As I tried to distance myself, I could feel a wad of spit directed my way. As much as it would sting on the inside, as much as those insults would stick with me the entire day, I looked back solely at Remi and tried to leave, without thinking about what had just been said to me.

The whole group of those degenerates began to erupt in laughter. It was as if they knew I would not respond or do anything to counter what had just been said to me.

All they wanted was a cheap shot to tame their masculinity, or the premature stages of it.

As I continued to make my way out, I looked back at Remi once more.

"How about a little respect, shitheads?"

I cringed in that very moment. What had he done? I had always tried to avoid these situations, yet he was about to engage in a violent conversation with kids no older than 15?

I questioned his confidence. He wasn't going to throw hands, was he?

The whole place fixated their glance at us. I made a frantic signal to Remi, we needed to leave immediately. Was it too late? had he already engaged in a fight with these kids?

They looked back, in a glance of shock. As if they had not seen someone give a rebuttal like this before.

"And what are you going to do lard ass?"

His voice was deep, but it was the kind I would expect from a boy that age and size.

"Remi let's just leave". God, I sounded like an obsessed girlfriend, trying to stop her brute boyfriend from a fight.

At this point, no words could stop him. In a torrent of rage, he lunged toward the hoodlum. A large gasp could be heard from the patrons, who proceeded to move out of the way as he continued his charge. I, who stood close to the glass door, cringed at the sight.

He eventually got a hold of the boy and held him in a headlock. For the only thing I could do was watch, like the bystander I was. The boy scrambled to get out of his grasp, but Remi held firm. I wanted to call out, stop him from possibly embarrassing himself further, but at the same time, I could not be caught in the crossfire.

A blurred mess of screams, gasps and heckling were visible to me as I continued to watch instead of doing anything. I did not know Remi could do something as cruel as this. I started breathing heavily, as those kids continued to berate Remi with insults.

"Let me go you fat fuck", he sounded suffocated as he struggled to get the words out.

I stood there, frozen in time as he continued to suffocate this child. He showed no remorse, no sympathy for that teenage prick. I couldn't say I wasn't impressed.

"You like that you fucking gutter rat?"

In a split second, the boy broke free, and punched Remi, dragging him across the entire floor of the establishment. His friends had now joined in, trying to pummel Remi across the floor of the place. A flurry of workers and members of the public swarmed the scene, as all I could do was watch like the imbecile I was. My heart rate could not be contained, Remi had just done something unfathomable for 'people' like us.

I wanted him to stop, but at that moment, a man intervened and manhandled Remi away from the boy.

"Call the police on this monster"

I could do nothing but stand there, like an idle sheep in disgust and horror. The hoodlum was still in shock at the sheer power he possessed. Bleeding from his mouth, he touched it once to check what had happened.

The man who stopped this ordeal stared Remi deep in the face. Everybody was shocked at what had just happened. Not just him.

"Ricardo. Let's get out of here"

He looked at me, so did everybody else. A wave of cringe and embarrassment emanated throughout my entire body as he looked. Immediately, I felt resentment for myself for even asking to meet him at a place like this. This was Remi Palludan after all. Could I have just told him over the phone? I didn't know whether to thank him or scold him for what he had done anyways. He did this for me after all. I had always been cautious when talking to Remi. He had an aura about him that made him seem threatening. This only bolstered that feeling.

Everyone continued staring at me, suitcase in hand, as I immediately beelined toward the exit. I needed to get out of there as soon as possible. I imagined Remi wanted to aswell. He pushed the chair he knocked down to the ground out of the way, and left the mess he had created. All the while, the older gentleman frantically spoke to the police, slurring his words in his description of Remi. In that moment, the entire room felt a sense of weariness.

THE WORLD'S REVENGE

REMI PALLUDAN, 23 JUNE 2009

I will continue to write. I need the world to understand my pain and suffering. I had always been told I was special. That feeling only multiplied when I bought the firearm. My family still couldn't bear the fact that I was incapable of getting a regular job now, also the fact that I didn't care anymore. I had been radicalised, in ways that even now, cannot be fixed. It had been approximately 3 months since that fateful night, the night my entire life took a turn for the worst. My mental state has not yet recovered from that incident. Even now. It is for those reasons alone I will continue to write. I will continue to show the reader my sullen, doomed life so that no one can repeat it. This account is a tragedy. A tragedy that cannot be replicated. The world, society has committed a great deal of injustice to me, the likes of which I can never return. So, I ask the reader, to learn from my tragedy, to learn that society is against me. For it has happened. I have been radicalised.

Yes, I do have pain etched deep inside my heart. That cannot be changed. But every human needs a companion. For me, the feeling of sex was something I had not yet experienced. At the age I was at the time, in my twenties, that was unheard of. Especially in the degenerate cesspit of the states. Throughout my teenage years I would hear stories of people having sexual relations, only to dream of one day doing such a thing myself. At the time, I would imagine myself and Meredith, living a fulfilled life together, shrouded in love, and of course sex. But that dream has gone. So has all hope of me being able to become a loving husband, father and son. It seemed everywhere I would turn, the women on the street would clammer in disgust. Stories on how I attempted to touch Meredith must have circulated, alongside pictures of my face.

It was for this reason I had become radicalised. I had no intention of living a life of peace and 'tranquillity'. Nor was this possible anymore. I had to be 'different'. Society had now forced me. My life had now become a tale of starvation and yearning. I wanted a job, but that was near impossible with my record. Especially if you were classed as a 'sex offender'.

With all the hatred I have for women, I equally have a sense of longing for the female touch. Doing such a thing to Meredith was likely no accident on my end. I continued to fantasise about what had transpired every night. Despite the sheer embarrassment I felt during the scenario, I usually calmed myself down usually by reimagining that same soft, enigmatic touch. The folds on her skin, the tight fit of her dark black dress, and the way my hands penetrated that thin layer of fabric, the way her hips swayed, her face – the perfect build for any woman, and her celestial smile. For those three gruelling months, in which I was brutally cut off from society, and cut off from living a happy life, bringing myself back to the memory always provided a sense of comfort. But this would be short lived. Knowing that there was a man, ten times my size most likely having

sex with her made my blood boil every time I would think about it. Invading that beautiful build, planting his lips on her beautifully sculpted face, pushing his abnormally large member inside of her. I could not
fathom the fact that such a thing was even happening at all. Around this time period, I tried to branch out, and possibly find love elsewhere. I could no longer bear the stares and the heckling constantly being thrown towards me every waking second. My radical mind wanted revenge, yes. But at the same time, I was desperate for a companion. I could not rid myself of the curse that was male sexuality. It was for that very reason I decided to move to the outskirts of Las Vegas, around the Henderson area. I felt this would be the perfect opportunity to start a new life, away from those imbeciles that would wish death upon me every single time they would stare deep inside my broken soul. How wrong I was back then.

This was a desperate bid to save my ever-worsening sanity, and show me that women were in fact, humble beings.

I decided, in a fit of desperation, that I would pitch the idea of me moving there to my parents. I conceived it as a 'new beginning' to them, whilst also talking about finding of a job there. That was what really caught their attention.

Of course, I was in no rush to find employment whilst I was there. I thought if I could experience the feeling of sex once, I would truly enact revenge. Of course, still holding the naïve thought that women were sentient beings.

My parents were starstruck by what I had pitched to them. I, Remi Palludan, finding a job, as well as living by himself? Even now, that reality seems distant – not true. I proceeded to then make the humble request of financial help from my parents and they, just as naïve as I back then, jumped at the opportunity to provide financial security. Offering to pay for the first few months of rent on my new place. I began scouring for places to stay there. I wanted to go with the cheapest options, eventually settling on a shared apartment complex called Peace Waters. It was a scenic place, tons of green space and a crisp lake right beside it. The perfect place for a person like me to thrive. Or so I thought. It took a couple days, a week at most, for my parents to finalise the place. I wasn't entirely sold on the idea of sharing a living space with other people, but in my torrent of desperation and heartbreak, anything was possible. I still could not get that whore out of my head. Meredith. The very recollection of her name would anger me to horrific levels. Her perfect body, her waist, her face. They were all meant for me, and me alone.

But after managing to finalise my move to Henderson, I believed that this curse that had been inflicted on me since that very day would finally dissipate. I would finally be able to live a happy, fulfilled life I saw all those men live when I would take those walks of depression in the park.

I would forget about that incident straight away. Once I experience the feeling of myself upon a female body, by any means necessary. This was the last time I would ever feel a sense of excitement for the future. A feeling that has been lost as my life faded even more into obscurity.

By now, you must know that I am an irrational being. It is just as big a curse as my crippling desire for sex. That's where women have us men cornered. I knew that all of this was a huge fit of rage and insanity from me. The suburb around the place wasn't too bad either. Just what I had expected from a manufactured 1950s suburban wasteland. What mattered most at this point was my ability to start a new life, a life that I knew I deserved. All the suffering I was forced to endure would now come to an end. At least that was what I needed to believe.

In a matter of weeks, I had packed my things and felt ready to begin this new chapter, filled with purpose and excitement. My parents had agreed to pay the bills for the first two months, and I figured I could get a job in that period, whilst also potentially finding true love in a scenic, crisp new environment. However, looking back it was only a continuation of the tragedy that was my life.

On the day of my big move, I made sure I looked my best going into this 'shared apartment'. Who knew if there would also be girls in the same complex as me? Just knowing that simple fact would fill me with all forms of excitement. I was ready to give my confidence another shot.

It was 9 hours from San Francisco to Las Vegas, we decided to stop off at Bakersfield to catch our breath and replenish ourselves for another couple hours of driving. The journey lasted a while, but once we arrived at Henderson, it was even better than what I had seen in pictures. The area, a typical 1950s suburban town, with manufactured streets and houses dotted along the street. Young couples around my age walked across the almost barren streets, carrying an envious sense of confidence a person like me lacked heavily. I held a sullen hope in my mind that one of those couples would be me in the next months. But now, knowing the true motives of those vermin we call women, I scoff at the fact I even thought of such a notion. The 9-hour car journey really did take a toll on me, the hair that I had been so proud of when walking out of the house was now a dishevelled mess, made worse by the fact I hadn't showered when we stopped off at Bakersfield.

I was deluded, and I failed to see that.

How I wish I could go back and tell myself that there was no usage in trying. The optimism I had was almost saddening to reminisce about. But I was ready, to start this new chapter in Las Vegas. I chose Las Vegas as it was the capital of all things I needed. I wanted a female partner, and I knew that women in Vegas would practically throw themselves at anyone. As I didn't perceive myself as attractive, I assumed that every woman would be looking for some form of sex with any male they could get their hands on.

Yet again, another example of my deluded brain.

I lacked all forms of socialisation with women up until that point. Yes, I had talked with them here and there, but I had never sustained a deep, thought-provoking conversation with them. Nor did I want to. The only thing I had to attain and needed at this moment was sex. Nothing else.

I did have an interest in getting to know a woman, and potentially starting a family. But even back then, I knew this was nothing more than fallacy.

My parents managed to drop me off at 'Peace Waters', or just outside the entrance. My father accompanied me to the leasing office, I saw a faint smile form in his face when they handed me the keys to the apartment. In an odd sense, it felt as if they wanted me out. I couldn't complain anyways, who would want a doomed human being such as I? He didn't know that this was all some twisted effort to gain some form of purpose and sexual interaction in my life. Not even I could think of doing something like this.

The apartment was only a few short blocks away, situated after going up two flights of steps. The place was a shithole, even to my standards. The lights upon the stairs flickered as you would walk past them, the dotted blue carpet on the stairs had mysterious brown stains on them and the smell was one I, nor my father had ever come across before. At this point, I wasn't feeling too optimistic.

The apartment number read 17B, with the silver plating almost chipping off from the door.

I was then introduced to three new housemates, one being a man named Lyota, a tall Asian guy. I could immediately tell that he had the privilege of female attention, judging from his attractiveness. I couldn't say I wasn't jealous, his build clearly far more superior than mine. His hair was probably enough to get all those fucking chicks obsessing over him. The other guy, whose name was too complex for me to remember also screamed of female attraction. His chiselled jawline, coupled with his long, surfer like blonde hair also felt like a punch in the face to my so-called attractiveness, I felt like a fool for even assuming I looked decent in the first place. And there I stood, running on a couple hours of sleep and overweight, with my hair going in several different directions. I was clearly inferior.

The last housemate however, I was in no way prepared for. Just as I thought that this would be a masculine slug fest, another person emerged from a room in the far back of the corridor. A girl. She had distinctive luscious blonde hair, with her tanned legs and thighs on display from her shorts. I felt her feminine aura captivate me in ways that bitch Meredith did not. Her name was Lenora, quite fitting for the radiance of light she emanated simply from being there. She looked like the type I would heckle and slut shame in my college days, but something was different about her. Something, I couldn't pinpoint. She was beautiful, but I knew a slob like me would not be able to talk to her, let alone allowing her to provide me with sexual pleasure. It was almost as if she had no imperfections, none that I could envision with my eyes.

We quickly unpacked in the room I would be staying in; it was nice enough for the time being. The curtains did have some mystery orange stains on them, and the bedsheets looked slightly discoloured, but nothing that would significantly hinder my existence here. We headed out for dinner at a restaurant in a somewhat upscale establishment downtown before my parents sent me on my way.

I arrived back to this apartment filled with optimism. The first night there was anything but optimal, however. The bed was creaky, made noises every time I would move even an inch. The walls felt paper thin, succumbing to every single minuscule noise that would come from the other rooms. I was in a room directly next to Lenora, and I could quite clearly hear her talking to what seemed like her boyfriend. Judging from the fact that they were talking about sex every few sentences, it was obvious. I held a little bit of hope that she was different. But knowing the cruel, vile essence of women now, I was a fool for making that assumption. The torture of listening to her speaking seductively to anyone other than myself was sickening. The fact that the walls were so poorly designed as much as to let me hear her moan through the phone was mind crushing. I tried to bury my ears in the stained pillow, but that didn't do much in fixing things. Her voice was angelic and soft, exciting to simply listen to, but it was tarnished and stained by what she was speaking about.

I feared. I feared that my time here would be wasted with the torture of women rejecting me, as they always had done before. I tried silencing those voices, but I couldn't. My sorrow mind only wanted sex, and I intended to achieve it immediately.

My only problem was women. Those pieces of vermin have no perception of reality. A gentleman like me is never valued anymore. Overhearing that blonde beauty speak such vulgar and seductive words was the reality of my first few nights in Vegas. It didn't help that the city was infested with young couples around my age. If only Meredith had accepted my advances. I too could have been in the same position. I should have known then that love was and always will be fake.

It also didn't help that my other housemates would bring back girls almost every night. And with that, came horrific torture in the form of bed creaking and moaning directly through the thin wall. Some days, it would be too much. I would often cry through the brown stained pillow, only intensifying my hatred for women entirely. I went to this place to rid my mind of Meredith, but all I got was more pain every single night, still shellshocked from the incident. My parents also couldn't support me anymore financially. All I was left with was guilt, and sadness. At that point, I was convinced that nothing could save me anymore. Nothing under the sun would allow me to indulge in pleasures others from my age group had seen such success in. I remember trying to drown out those sorrows by heading down to a casino only a 5-minute walk away from my apartment complex. It was the only place I could really think and have 'fun'. The endless cycle of the slot machines and the bright colours all over the place, gave me a false sense of happiness. One that was temporary.

I knew that sooner or later, I would need to find a job, or move out having accomplished nothing. I knew my time here wasn't ideal, but I needed to make the most out of a painful situation.

I would spend the little money I was given in the casino and get black out drunk whilst doing so. The casino was connected to a bar, and it was there I would drink away the sorrows of my existence.

But my drunken adventures would often lead to devastating tirades right after. I got into fights more times than I could count, swinging at guys twice my age, sometimes smashing the glass bottle of alcohol I would have in my grasp. It was a good way to relieve all that tension I had stored inside of me, but even then I knew that someday I would lose all sense of control.

Nothing would have prepared me for the day I finally cracked. I was down to my last 50 bucks, and with that money, I went about my usual business, walking down to the casino, and proceeding to spend the next few hours having a go at the slot machines, then later move to the bar in which I would drink, relieving myself of all the tension of the slot machines I would spend hours on. But this night, something in the air felt different. Almost every man I would see was with a woman of some sort, which wasn't a good occurrence in the first place. Not only that, but a lot of them were kissing right next to me, or it felt as such. This already soured my mood as I moved to the bar. I was already on edge, but I hoped that drinking heavily would ease those feelings. I sat there, at the bar, when a man approached me, half drunk. His face was flushed, and he couldn't look or move straight. I wasn't exactly clean either, but it was clear he had been at it for a while.

"I would beat you the fuck up". He said, with his drunken stutter. Usually, I would brush off these comments, as I would have some level of sanity. But this night, was different. The fact that I was practically broke, spending my last dollars on cheap shots, watching people kiss in what was, my place of serenity was probably a big factor why.

He looked around, probably just stunned, but I personally couldn't take it anymore. I grabbed my shot glass and clubbed it on his wad of frizzy hair. It probably didn't do much, but it stimulated some sort of barbaric drunken response from him.

His fist came in from the right, but I was experienced enough to narrowly avoid it. His drunken state made him telegraph a lot of his movements before he enacted them. My pure driven anger, coupled with my semi light-headedness, made me a beacon of rage. I grabbed his striped buttoned shirt and directed my fist at his stomach. His groan when my fist landed gave me a strong indication, I had done something. Yet, at the same time I felt my hair almost disconnecting from my scalp as the drunken beast pulled it, holding nothing back. I glanced up for a split second to see his hairy knuckles cascade across my face as I fell to the ground, with my hair still stinging from when he pulled it. I tried my best to recover and arise back, but at that point, it was too late. I felt him pummel me from all angles, as I rushed to cover up. By then, the whole world turned into a blurry slowed down mess, and the only things I could hear were the screams from a woman.

"Joel, Joel, stop it. You're too drunk, stop"

A woman grabbed this brute's fists before he could hit me further. I wallowed there, helpless. Just as helpless as I was when the Samoan was raining down hell. I knew this was all Meredith's fault. That fucking whore. I couldn't do anything. My rage was yet to be unleashed. I screamed and got up, charging at this piece of scum, but I was no match for the security, who formed a barrier between me and the drunk dog. I clenched my fists and gnashed my teeth. I would drink to drown out my unhappiness, but that day, drinking was the sole factor to my downfall.

It didn't stop there, however. I made my way out of the cesspit, and drunkenly walked back to 'Peace Waters'. My feet were planting themselves in all sorts of different directions, as I struggled to make my way back. My mind turned into a flurry every step I would take, despite only being at the bar for 30 minutes. The lights that shone from cars looked like beacons, shooting up into the sky. I needed to try my hardest to keep myself upright, constantly looking down at my feet to steady myself.

I touched my lip for a split second and looked at the blood I had drawn from that fight. I felt weak, and this was charged by that woman having to stop that beast from hurting me.

It took a good while for me to eventually get back to the apartment, I could barely get up the stairs, and had to walk on all fours just to gain a sense of balance. My hands would tremble as I tried inserting the key inside, missing the hole numerous times.

I needed some way to release these frustrations I had. Losing a fight to a drunk pig hadn't cooled my mood in the slightest. And this place only made things worse.

I opened the door to find the corridor, pitch black. I was too drunk to turn on the lights, nor did I want to. It was 1AM on a Saturday, so I had assumed all the people in the house were out. But I was partially right. The only person in the house appeared to be Lenora. Her lights were on, and her door was left slightly ajar.

I suddenly felt a rush of sexual energy, the likes of which I had not experienced before. I could suddenly feel my head stopping spinning, and I could feel my teeth gnash, just as it did the bar. In that moment, I felt like a lion, having newly found his prey. I looked around once more, this was the first time, I was in a house alone with a woman. Looking back, I have no regrets of what I was about to do. I removed my shoes and made my way inside her room. Her room was filled with trinkets, a blue wallpaper, and blue bedsheets. Much more dignified than my pigsty across the corridor. She looked at me, shocked that I had done such a thing, and questioned my drunken appearance.

"Uh, do you need something?" I could hear her voice echo as my dizziness didn't stop.

Her hair looked slightly untamed, but nothing could have taken away from her perfect face. She continued staring at me, as if I had done something sinister. That however, was yet to come.

"Do you need something?" she kept saying it. It had no meaning. There was no one in this house. Nothing to stop me. I knew I had the dominance over this girl. It was a scenario I could only see going one way. I could not waste this opportunity to fulfil my primal desires. It was time. I let out a sinister smile and looked back. Did she know what I was about to do? I could not make out what she said, but I could remember her hands trembling, squirming for a phone on the desk. Her words soon became infested with fear. Even in my drunken state, I could sense it. It was the perfect opportunity. I leaned in toward her and grabbed her two hips. Just as I had done with Meredith. I quickly shut the door; I did not want to hear her screams any longer. I could hear my breaths and began to sweat. This forceful release of sexual desire and tensions could not wait, I had little time before something would happen.

I dragged her by those hips and forcefully pushed her onto her blue coloured bed. I could see the black streaks of tears protrude from her eyes. There are seldom occurrences I would feel 'guilt'. But this, was one of those occurrences. I held her two soft, manicured hands in place. Her radiance still permeated despite the ordeal she found herself in.

I reduced her down to her bare body and took one second amongst the chaos to observe and decipher the enigma of the female. I touched her breasts. they were soft, squishy to the touch almost. My sexual energy doubled every time I would lay a finger on them.

"Please. Stop"

I could feel a connection, I could feel our bodies mesh. I was sweaty throughout it, but her body gave me such joy and comfort I could not stop, despite her moving all over the place.

"Please. Stop"

Those sweet, soft cries spurred me on. Her voice was so pure, so innocent, I forgot completely about her late-night phone conversations, in which she would say such unspeakable things. I could not stop. I would never stop, until I felt a rush of energy, which combined with a sharp thrust from my body onto hers. I let out a groan and gnashed my teeth as I could feel fluid rush inside of her. She screamed as she could feel the fluid ooze inside, squirming on the bed, whilst I completed my journey of pleasure.

She began to breathe heavily. But now, she stopped trying to push me off her. She stopped trying to wrestle her way out. She annoyed me. Her constant squirming, her lack of submission made it a rather mindless task. If only Meredith had also submitted to my desires, maybe this poor girl would not have had her dignity snatched away from her.

My breathing subsided, I tried to control it. I handed back her clothes and touched her soft, dishevelled hair one last time. She struggled to breathe after what had just happened. I placed her blue duvet over her naked body and made my way out of the room. I knew now that I was in a race against time. My drunken body quickly grabbed my brown bag from the top of the dresser and filled it with my clothes. I knew that I had done something unthinkable, but the thrill of losing my virginity was the only thing that came to mind at that point.

I could hear those soft, futile cries coming from her room. I stopped placing clothes in the bag for one second and took a deep breath. Unfortunately for her, this was something that needed to be done. Women had rejected me for too long, insulted me for my appearance and personality. I needed to relieve that stress. So, it was then, at the age of 24, I finally managed to crawl out of the shell that was being a virgin. I still hated women, however. My revenge would be incomplete if I did not do something as abhorrent to Meredith. I needed to.

But I need to admit, hearing that girl's wailing from the other room provided me with some twisted form of pleasure. I grabbed the shoe box in which I had stored my guns and held them whilst blowing the dust off. Another twisted thought came to mind as I thought of blowing a bullet past her. I initially enjoyed the sounds of her cries from the other room, but upon realising what I had just done, I needed to act quick. Even a being such as I could not just kill someone in cold blood. Her body was a vessel for me to relieve my pleasure. That was the assumption I had.

I had little to no compassion for the girl whose life I had ruined. She merely provided me an insight to the pleasures others had enjoyed at my expense. I needed to get out of there quick, before I would be beat to a pulp by my housemates. Knowing and hearing the conundrum of wailing coming from the other room worried me, as I wasn't exactly the 'social' type. I barely spoke to any of my housemates, including Lenora before I used her for my sexual pleasure. I dreaded what would happen if the other guys were to come back and discover the state the girl was in. So I continued to frantically grab my belongings, despite being a drunk dog. I carefully placed my guns in a separate compartment in the bag and lifted it upright. The time was 2AM. I could faintly hear something coming from Lenora's room. She had stopped crying minutes earlier, but I could faintly hear her on the phone.

She was calling the police.

I dropped my bag for one second and clambered my fists. Still, with zero regrets upon what I had just committed, I quickly opened my bag once more, and grabbed the gun I had stored within it.

I needed a moment to look at it and admire its beauty. I questioned myself, did I need to do this?

Hearing her dial and speak to the police worried me, I knew I would be finished if they were to find me. But I couldn't bring myself to fill her with lead.

My mind now became a war, debating itself whether to let the girl live or not. I kept hold of the weapon, turning it around in my palm, fidgeting with it. If I wanted to kill her, I needed to do it soon before the pigs arrested me. I planted my palms in my face. I needed to decide, for my own safety. I couldn't go to prison. Despite the prospect of my life being over, I needed freedom. I had been sitting in my dump of a room for about 10 minutes, contemplating. I had a good feeling she had dialled the police, and my distinct drunken appearance would no doubt put me in danger. I knew that this gun was my only source of power. My only way of getting out of this predicament.

Even I could not do it. I grabbed my bag and waddled over to the door. I took a quick glance back at Lenora's room. She had shut it tight, and I could hear her on the phone, to the police. I hurried over back to the door and shut it audibly. I knew now that I was a fugitive. And so, my attempts to start a 'new life' in Vegas was spoiled, and only brought a crippling addiction to gambling and a potential rape charge.

I had no regrets upon what I had just done to this girl. Yes, I did feel some remorse, but in the end the adrenaline and the pleasure of hearing her cries unleashed a primal feeling. And I knew, that if I were to come face to face with Meredith, I would do the same deed, and have the courage to shoot her afterward. My drunken pain did not subside as I made my way down the stairs. I had nowhere to go, with 25 dollars in my bank account, I could not hitch a ride back to San Francisco. My heartbeat tripled as I wandered onto the street, depleted of energy and purpose.

I thought that forcing myself upon that girl would help my desire. If anything, it only tripled that primal instinct. I wished to do the same to Meredith. To make her feel the same pain and suffering Lenora felt whilst I unleashed my fury upon her.

DESIRE

I spent a few nights crashing at Remi's house.

The house itself was unlike anything I had seen before. The blank white walls and unopened boxes scattered around the place led me to assume he had just moved in. Once again, I had nowhere to go.

In those few days, me and Remi did just about everything together. After being disowned, it felt as if all doors had shut themselves on me, but after spending these few days with Remi, I could really feel a sense of brotherhood, the likes of which I only saw from other people. I still had the money I had kept, just in case things were to go south.

I told Remi all about my dysfunctional household, he seemed to understand where I was coming from. It was relieving, having him reassure me.

Things went 'normal' in a sense, until a few days later, when he came late at night, with a crooked step.

"Hey man, you want to order a whore?"

He sounded drunk, so I didn't take him seriously. He shut the door and fell onto the recliner that was placed in the corner of the room. He wanted to order a prostitute.

I knew he had a deep hatred for women, I couldn't say I wasn't worried about what would happen.

I decided to look back at him, I had an inquisitive look in my eye.

"You mean a prostitute?"

It seemed that was what he was talking about as he reached for his phone in his drunken state.

He nodded as he would proceed to dial a number on his phone. It seemed like he had experience with ordering women.

"But I thought you hated women" I asked him.

He chuckled and stopped dialling for a second.

"Listen Ricardo. Women aren't emotionally smart beings. But we men, need some form of pleasure. We need sex. We spend half of our life longing for the female touch. Those whores are only good for one thing. To satisfy the male's intricate feelings of desire which we cannot get rid of"

He sounded drunk, but still articulate in the words he used. Plus, I was still a virgin, after all. He looked at me and asked the same thing. "Are you a virgin?"

It looked like he was almost about to laugh. One could tell from my mannerisms and appearance that I never got any women. I also knew that a man's worth was decided by how many women he managed to seduce and fuck. I felt weak, as he stopped to dial the number again. I didn't get the hint that Remi wasn't a virgin anyways. This was the one time I now felt jealous of him. I didn't even know I could be jealous of a being such as him. How did he lose his virginity? I felt inclined to ask. I waited for him to finish speaking on the phone and posed my question.

"So, how did you lose your virginity then?"

Suddenly, his face turned from flushed to a light red colour. He gave me a stare, the type of stare that a killer would make before he severed his victim.

"You don't want to know, Ricardo. All you should know is that I am not a virgin." He said. "Now we wait."

I decided to hold back from asking any wayward questions, but I sunk in my seat. I knew Remi was someone I feared subconsciously, but this only bolstered that feeling. I had a strong assumption that he had lost his virginity through deviant means.

"You ready to lose your virginity then?" He asked.

"I guess so" I replied.

I had no idea that today would be the day I would finally be pleasured by a woman. Despite the woman being a prostitute. I sunk in my seat as I waited on Remi's fake leather chair, with cotton emerging out of the multiple holes within it. I never knew or anticipated this would be the occasion I longed for. Part of me wished that I had found someone the 'traditional' way, but at this point, the mere prospect of feeling a woman's body was enough for someone like me.

I felt an odd sense of nervousness, as I sat there, waiting. I looked at Remi's clock, being one of the only things he had hung up on the blank white wall. The sound it made when it would tick, almost like a bullet piercing through the skin. Remi sat there, unfazed with a blank expression written all over his face. I always imagined I would find a loving wife, who would provide me with all the sexual pleasures I needed, but it was no secret that I wanted sex now.

"Do you want to fuck her first?" He said, trying to strike up a conversation to break the awkward silence. If anything, that made this wait a little more awkward.

I stroked my elbow and placed my clenched fist near my mouth. Did I really want to have sexual intercourse with a woman I didn't know first?

Soon enough, I heard a knock on the door. My heart began doing circles as Remi glanced at me, with a smirk on his face. Did I want to go first?

"Looks like your life is about to change" he said. "I'll answer the door". He arose from his seat to get the door, as I sat there, trying to brace myself. I thought losing my virginity would be a little more dignified. I would never have imagined I would lose it in a damp, cold apartment in a sketchy neighbourhood.

The door opened, and I could have my first sight of the woman Remi had asked for. Her hair was a monstrosity, coupled with the fact that the skin on her face had drooped down and amalgamated a beast, the likes of which even I would turn down. Despite my urge to feel the touch of a woman, I could not have intercourse with her. Her bestial appearance made me refuse to even lock eyes with her, let alone feel a genuine connection.

"Ricardo, this is Florence"

I managed to get a better look at the beast as Remi stepped back from the door. She looked confused, constantly looking back at Remi with an expression of genuine disgust.

"So you want me to do him?" she said.

Remi shut the door, and in his drunk state he let out a short chuckle, as if this had been a huge joke.

"Why can't you do both of us you fucking slut"

The words he used shocked even me, who knew the extent of his antics. As expected, she looked back with a shocked expression written all over her face. He wasn't lying, but maybe his drunken state didn't help things. She moved a step closer to the door. She probably thought she was in danger of some sort. Even though she was the ugliest slut I had laid eyes upon, I could not help but feel sorry for her.

"You gotta pay extra if you want me to fuck both of you"

Seemed like a reasonable offer. She seemed a little rattled from the comment, but I knew Remi would not take this lightly.

"Fuck me first, and we'll see" he said. I was hoping that he wasn't going to do anything too rash. Even he probably knew.

It seemed like he had no spatial awareness as he started stripping in the middle of the room, irrespective of the fact that I was still sitting there. The whore also played along with it. She took a quick glance at me, and proceeded to remove the black corset she had been wearing. As she did, I caught sight of a tattoo she had on her arm. It was the only tattoo she had on her arm and it read 'Samoa' in thick black ink. Whoever had done the tattoo didn't do that well of a job either, as ink was protruding away from the word.

Remi was probably too drunk to even acknowledge another guy was there, or he might have wanted me to feel some sort of way upon seeing him fuck a prostitute. They continued to remove their clothes regardless. Florence was hesitant, as she kept looking back at me before removing her undergarments. I had seldom experienced such a level of awkwardness in a room before now, as she stood there unfazed, opening her dotted bra to reveal her scaly figure. From looking at both Remi and Florence's bodies together, it was amusing to see that Remi had bigger breasts than her. I could tell that Florence had a thin figure, but once she removed her clothes, I got that feeling multiplied tenfold. The room was completely silent. The only sounds that could be heard were the rustling of their clothes being removed. Remi tossed his clothes aside, and his body was on full show. He had stretch marks dotted across his torso, with hair sticking out of his nipples like live wires.

"Get down". He said to the whore.

She obliged, as her naked body began to kneel and instinctively, she grabbed his loin as she went down there. His pubic hairs were also unshaved, but his towering stomach fat probably masked the monstrosity of a bush he had stored down below. Florence's thin lips latched onto the loin, just how a magnet attracts metal. She was a slut, after all. She knew just how to extract the raw pleasure out of a man. It seemed to be working, as the sucking sounds were equally met with Remi's moans. It almost made me chuckle, the way he let loose in that moment. I stayed, in the corner of the room watching on as the woman tamed Remi, sucking the living daylights out from within him. I could feel myself getting harder, to the point of no return. Remi's moans intensified, and that whore kept on sucking. She couldn't and wouldn't stop, despite the wad of pubic hair he kept untamed. I was a mere bystander, as I always had been, watching my new 'friend' getting pleasured by a slut.

Both of their breathing intensified. They both started breathing in sync. I could not believe what I was witnessing. The breathing came to a standstill, with now only Remi letting out a couple extra moans to finish it off.

He proceeded to remove his member from her mouth and grabbed some tissues from the table next to him. I was a man aswell, a frail shell of a man, but a man nonetheless. I knew exactly what was going on in his mind at that moment. One of the many lessons I had learnt throughout my years of sullen, depraved life was that pleasure comes at a price. Remi began to immediately wear his clothes again, probably ashamed of what he had just done. Was I up next?

"Are you going to fuck my friend here now?" He said, waving at me as if I were something disposable. "I'll pay you extra".

It's almost as if he wanted me to be fucked by this slut. She clearly felt uncomfortable in this environment. Who wouldn't be, when two men are in the room, having just sucked the life out of a man.

"Listen, I would but I just don't feel like it right now" she said. I would happily accept that response, but Remi would not take no for an answer. It looked like he wanted me to lose my virginity, badly. He let out an audible laugh. I had the feeling he was not going to let her go this easily.

"You are a fucking slut. Just fuck him it's not that hard."

He was more desperate than I was to fuck someone. After he managed to put his clothes back on, he shut the door and fastened the chain lock. After seeing what had transpired the other day, I had no doubt he wasn't going to change his mind.

The slut stayed there, silent as I tried to lock eye contact with her. Deep down, even I did not want to do this.

She let out a deep sigh. Before her eyes began to water, almost beginning to cry.

"I have a family, a son."

"I don't give a fuck" Remi replied. "You're not making it out without fucking him". He pointed towards me as he said it. He stood by the door, making sure she could not exit the room, and kept pointing at me.

She didn't utter a single word as she undressed once more.

"Remi, I can't do this" I said. Forceful sex was not the type I was remotely interested in. Yet, Remi didn't seem to take it lightly.

"Just fuck her. I'm going to watch."

Florence stopped removing her clothes. She knew I was not going through with this.

He laughed, again.

"A whore not fucking someone for money. This is new". He said.

"Women have feelings, Mr Palludan" she said. "I really don't feel like having sex back-to-back"

Remi laughed once more. This time, the laugh felt forced.

"You think me, or my boy here care about your feelings? No one gives a shit, darling. Just screw the guy, it's not hard".

She looked back at me, once more to evaluate my facial expression. My face told her everything she needed to know. The feeling of cringe coupled with the fact that I was being forced gave me a sour, nervous look.

"Just let me go, please". She spoke. I could tell Remi was getting restless, whilst I was still processing what was going to happen. He grabbed a suspicious looking box right next to the door and opened it. Me and the slut both looked on in shock and anticipation.

Knowing Remi, I knew that this would potentially be dangerous. And low and behold, it was. He pulled out a pistol of some sort, and cocked it. I could see a smile forming as he played with it, examining it as he then pointed it towards her. He was drunk. Anything could have happened.

"Fuck him. Now."

She immediately obliged. She had to now, her life and family were at stake.

She revealed her flat chested body to me once more and started walking towards me. In some twisted fashion, I felt relieved that my status as a virgin was about to be revoked. I quickly and hesitantly removed my clothes as well and looked at Remi once more. My heart was still pounding as he kept the gun locked on the girl.

She quickly surveyed my naked body, it was untamed and untouched, a swamp festering with pimples and hair sprouting from all angles. I wanted this over quick, I had too much empathy to refuse.

I looked down at my crotch for one final time. I was about to go all in. She lied down on the floor and spread her legs.

I took a deep breath. This was my first time, anyways. I had heard magical stories from other people about their first experiences, but nothing compared to doing it myself.

"So, do I just put it in?"

Remi nodded from across the room, as I tried to savour this moment, but couldn't. The girl looked too frightened to even enjoy it. As soon as I put it in, I felt a pillow of flesh wreathed upon my member. She felt warm, I could feel her shaking through her sharp breaths every time I would go in. Her legs were moving a little too much for my liking, but I went along with it regardless. I placed my hands on the floor, as I kept thrusting her lower body, forgetting the circumstances in which I managed to fuck her. I wanted to go in for a kiss, but I highly doubt she would let me. Feeling our two bodies intersect removed all the tensions I had experienced beforehand. I was breathing heavily, so was she. Every breath spoke a thousand words, as I tried to look into her eyes. Those eyes that carried so much burden.

We went at it for no less than 10 minutes before I felt that familiar sense of explosion. That sense of regret coupled with excitement. In that moment, I couldn't feel anything. I couldn't see anything; I couldn't move from my place as I excreted that all too familiar fluid. *Breathe.* I removed myself from the situation, caked in sweat. The slut also did the same, not saying a word as we kept her there. It was the earlier hours of the morning, the birds were beginning to sing, the sky changed colour from pitch black to a hue of blue, and Remi sat there, unfazed.

"Give me my money now". She sounded firmer, she had been crying the whole time I was trying to give it to her. Remi was now highly impatient, as he always was when he came back black out drunk and scoffed at her perceived suffering.

"You're really starting to piss me off".

It seemed she just wanted to get out of the place, as Remi kept waving his gun around, in a nonchalant fashion.

"For a dirty slut, you sure do have a lot of attitude". Remi said, in drunken fashion.

"Where's my money then". She said, with her hand out. I could see her hand trembling as it reached toward him. Once again, I saw the hand tattoo with the word 'Samoa' inscribed upon it.

"I'll give you your fucking money" Remi said. "Look at you. I'm surprised people pay you in the first place"

I looked up and tried to wait for this encounter to be over immediately. The post nut clarity had fully settled in at this point, and a feeling of regret set in on what I had just done. She was getting restless as well, I could feel it.

"Fuck you" she said. It looks like she managed to muster the courage to talk back. "I'm a fucking human at the end of the day, and you treated me like shit."

It felt like I was watching a deranged argument between a couple, but I feared for what Remi would do to this slut. She clearly had little regard for her own safety, by saying those words to someone with a gun pointed at them.

Remi smirked a little bit and played around with his gun once more. He grabbed it firmly and swerved back around to face her. Suddenly, he couldn't hold back anymore, and so fired a piercing bullet right in her chest. She let out a faint scream, whilst Remi began to take heavy breaths in his underwear. The pacing of his breaths fluctuated, as I stood there in utter shock. The bullet's residue cascaded, with blood rushing down the whore's chest area. I knew that her complacency would inevitably lead to this.

She began to breathe heavily in unison with Remi. Even she was in shock of what he had just committed. I saw her eyes roll back, as I came to terms with the fact that Remi had just killed a slut in front of me.

"We need to take her to a hospital" I said, in a fit of nervousness and panic. I rushed to cover her wound, feeling the slimy tenderness of her blood. "She- she can still live" I added, choking and slurring my words. I could hear her gasp for air. Remi let out a sigh, as if to condemn me for my concerns, and moved me out of the way. His strength overpowered mine, and so he pushed my chest away from her, and took a deep stare into her eyes. Blood continued to trickle down from her chest and Remi started to laugh. He walked through to his bedroom and a couple seconds later, pulls out a wad of 20-dollar bills stacked up and held together with a rubber band. He waved it at her, as if to tease her.

"Give this to your family slut". He continued to laugh; despite the services she had provided him.

He quickly threw the bills on the ground and fired two more shots. I covered my eyes, which didn't do much against the horror of her screams. He fired every single bullet he had in that gun and threw it on the ground. Florence now sported a mangled face, with her mouth covered with blood. Remi did this.

"I'm surprised a fucking whore like you even has a family"

He proceeded to kick her frail body to add to her suffering.

He threw the stack of money on her, before also spitting on her soon to be corpse.

"You see, Ricardo?" he said in an even more drunk manner. "Sluts like her don't deserve shit". He tried to shoot again, but the clip was completely empty. He threw the gun onto the floor and stared at the girl's dying moments.

"Remi, she had a family" I said. I struggled to keep it together against him.

"And she was a slut. The vermin of society. She deserved to die." The room continued to stay silent as the woman puked blood from her already bloodied face, spewing crimson red across the cheap porcelain floor. She coughed a small amount of blood for one second and fell headfirst onto the floor.

Her hair became a mop for her blood, that had now cascaded along the floor.

"How are we going to hide her body" I said. I was still fixated on her lifeless movements as she came to terms with her demise.

Remi touched her to confirm she was dead. He picked up the money he had callously dropped, and placed it on the table next to him.

Then he stood, lifeless.

It was as if he had switched off, unaware of the heinous crime he had just committed.

Suddenly, he turned back at me with a regretful, desperate stare in his eyes. His hands planted themselves onto his forehead and he began pacing in the room, constantly looking at the slut's dead body.

"Fuck, fuck fuck. Every fucking time. What the fuck have I done?" He kept repeating this, as he stared at her lifeless body.

I could physically feel my heart dropping to the deepest depths of my soul. I was in a situation I couldn't even conceive in my nightmares. A dead body inches away, and a 'friend' who came to an epiphany moments after. The image of the whore puking blood was now etched in my mind as Remi's eyes turned a bloodshot red.

"Fuck. She's dead, fuck" he said. "The neighbours must have heard those fucking gun shots"

With that, Remi now gave me a new reason to panic harder. He began pacing up and down his apartment, with the gun still on the floor.

"Why the hell did you kill her then?" I said in the nicest way I could come across. I didn't want to end up being his next victim. It seemed he didn't give two fucks about the boundary between friends.

"She deserved to die. But now there's a fucking mess I could get arrested for"

He kicked her head which had now fully absorbed the blood. Her forehead and face were fully dismembered from the multiple gunshots she had sustained. His pacing began to subside, before he eventually went into his room.

I heard rummaging sounds for a couple seconds, and he came out of the room wielding a brown suitcase, with checkered patterns across it.

"We need to put this slut's body in this" He said. "The cops might fucking show up any minute"

"Do it" he said.

My heart was doing laps as I bent down to collect her body.

"I do stupid shit when I'm drunk. Hell, I could commit a genocide For all I care" Remi said as I paused for a minute, refusing to collect the dead body.

Seeing her eyes rolled unto the back of her head, the blood still rushing out of her forehead covering the spots of dried blood on her flesh, it was a sickening sight. The likes of which I would not wish on the harshest of enemies.

"Pick the fucking body up goddamn" Remi said. He started to get restless. I clenched my fists as I viewed them for the last time in a clean state. They were about to endure in something far worse than masturbation.

I reached through the pool of blood to grab her back and lift her up. She was far lighter than I had anticipated, as I lifted her body and tried to stuff it inside the suitcase. I glanced up at Remi, who had just started heavily breathing again, holding his gun in his hands.

I placed the body over the suitcase, yet her lifeless legs and arms were still outside it.

Remi threw his gun on the ground, and grabbed her legs, trying to direct it into the suitcase once more.

"Fuck it, take her shoes off". I obliged, and grabbed those bright red shoes and threw them across the room. My hands were still bright red from handling her.

Remi then proceeded to stuff the body fully inside the suitcase and pressed on the girl's ribcage a couple times to make sure she was inside.

This was something unforeseen in my years of existence on this earth.

"Where are we going to put her body then?" I asked Remi, in a fit of panic and rage. That was the question, however. Where was she going to go?

In that moment, I knew that Remi Palludan was a murderer.

He managed to fully stuff the body inside the suitcase; pushing it to make sure it worked. He grabbed an extra clip for his gun and placed it inside. He tested it out, whilst I grabbed whatever clothes and belongings I had in the house. I knew that this would certainly be my last day here.

As I was stuffing my things into my suitcase, alongside the money I had stashed up, Remi approached me, with the body bag in his hand.

"We need to get the hell out of the state" he said. "Right fucking now".

I knew that something drastic needed to happen for us to get out of the predicament we were in, but moving out of the state was something that logically couldn't happen.

"How? You don't have a car" I said.

"We need to fucking steal one" he replied back. "We have no choice."

I dreaded at the thought of committing another crime. Thanks to Remi I was now reeled into a life I couldn't envision in a nightmare, let alone real life. Whose car were we going to steal?

"Your father has a car, yes or no?" he said.

My heart finally dropped down to the deepest depths of my body, to the point I could physically feel it.

"M-My father?" I spoke. I looked up at Remi for once, his hands still had the residue of blood on it.

"Yes, your father if you still have one"

I knew that my actual 'father' was a dead man, but my stepfather would kill me if I ever tried to step foot in that house. But this was a dire situation. I knew Remi had no regards for human life, he shot a prostitute for no logical reason.

"Ricardo, fucking listen to me" he said. I immediately looked up. I didn't want to be pierced by a bullet hole.

"My dad has a truck. Well, my stepfather anyway"

"That's perfect. We need to go now"

He ran to collect his gun, whilst I stood there in silence. I couldn't help but cry. Something catastrophic had just happened. And I now had no doubt, that something else was about to transpire.

TOUGH LOVE

We approached my house, only a few minutes away from where Remi was staying. Remi had his gun in his pocket. I dreaded to think what was going to happen when he had that. The body stayed in the apartment, as Remi said we needed to make a swift getaway.

"So, do you want me to ask him?" I said. I hoped we wouldn't do something too outlandish and drastic to him.

"Let's go inside first" he said. His menacing look didn't help my optimism in the slightest.

I realised I had gone too far with Remi to back out from his company.

"I won't do anything drastic Ricardo. There is nothing to be worried about" he said. "We just need to ask for the keys"

I knew my father wouldn't give the keys to the truck that easily. I could see the wretched thing, parked up on the driveway about 2 blocks down. Remi approached the house, and I followed, making sure I got in front of him.

I took multiple heavy breaths before knocking on that rusted door. It was 2 o clock in the morning. I didn't expect anyone to be up.

I looked up for a faint second, but as I did, there my father stood. Half asleep, and shocked at the sight.

"I told your useless ass to fuck off. What the fuck are you doing here, at this time?"

I tried holding my breath as I would say a word. But I was beaten to it by Remi.

"Listen fuckface, I don't give a shit about your relationship, we just want the car."

He hid his gun in his pocket. I held my breath and hoped he would not use it. Even I had some ounces of sympathy for my father.

"Give us the fucking car, before things get ugly" he said. I could tell when Remi was getting impatient, and this was one of those instances.

"Get off my property, before I call the cops". My father then proceeded to say. He shut the door on us, and to me I figured that was the end of it. But Remi Palludan had other ideas.

He kicked the door once and banged on the door. I curled up in fright, my heart was now doing laps around the place as I scanned to see if anybody was watching us.

My father opened the door once more, and took another good look at us.

"I'm calling the fucking cops. Ricardo, I don't know who this degenerate is, but I will have you and him arrested."

Remi laughed and pushed him inside. I needed to intervene.

"Remi, stop. Please. That's my father" I said. "Let's just catch a train or something"

Remi looked back at me, as if I were some sort of crackhead, and proceeded to keep my father pinned to the ground.

"We'll be fucking charged for murder at that rate, you fucking idiot" Remi said. It was the worst possible word he could have said in that moment, as my father heard everything.

"Ricardo? Who did you murder? Is my son a fucking killer?" he said, whilst staying pinned down on the ground. I couldn't help but release my emotions right there. I felt my eyes watering, and my legs began to go numb. Everything around me turned into a blurry mess, with voices around me.

Remi was now screaming. He was charged with the strongest rage I had ever seen from him. I realised I was being held hostage, with a mentally impaired recluse, who had no regard for other human's lives. I realised that it was for the best I didn't converse with him for months. But it was all wasted. I needed to comply, for my own safety.

"Your son is a fucking murderer, and what?" he said.

"He knows too much Ricardo; he knows too fucking much"

I was waiting for my mother to come out. She needed to. This was an active murder site. I was hoping her sleeping pills failed and she already called the cops. Somebody had to have done that.

I dreaded what would happen as Remi cocked his gun once more. I screamed "REMI STOP" as he pulled his gun towards him. I grabbed the gun, but to no avail. He pointed it directly at my father and looked at me before he did. It felt like he relished in seeing me, distressed.

"Last chance you old fuck. Give me the keys" he said.

He took a deep breath and probably swallowed his pride.

"They're behind me, on that rack"

Remi collected the keys, and kept his gun fixated on my father. I couldn't bear to look him in the eyes, I had too much guilt to answer for.

Remi walked towards the door, where I was stood. I could feel every step. The room then fell into a deep silence, with my father trying to stare at me whilst I tried to deny any eye contact with him. Remi looked at me for one second.

"You are a pussy aren't you? I'm sorry Ricardo, but he knows too much". He touched my rounded cheeks and turned around. My father was still on the floor, and he had just realised what was about to happen.

"Now turn around, and if you look at him, I'll shoot you aswell"

"Ricardo? Tell him to stop, tell your friend to stop. He's going to fucking shoot me, he's going to shoot" my father said. All whilst my mother was knocked out in the other room, I couldn't help but wail and cry at the sound of my father's screams for help.

"Ricardo? Help, FUCKING HELP"

"I'm your father, Ricardo, I'm your fucking father"

"I'm sorry, I'm sorry, just tell your friend to stop"

Remi found this amusing. That twisted fuck. He laughed at the sounds of my father's desperate pleas for help. My mind began to argue with itself, on whether I should sacrifice myself for a father who never loved me. His love only came at the most desperate times.

"Ricardo. I loved you, I love you. I only wanted what was best"

I had to help.

I turned around, despite the threat.

It was too late.

I couldn't save him.

As I did, I heard the silent, yet loud gunshot blow past his torso,

Leaving a gaping wound inside him.

Remi pulled me by the hand, and held the gun toward me.

He was still highly drunk, as his movements were nomadic and primitive. I needed to run toward my father, but Remi's sharp grasp held me tight.

I could see my father take his final breaths right in front of me, as Remi forced me to identify the truck.

"You're going to get us both arrested you pussy" he said. I couldn't care fewer what labels he applied to me. Soon enough, Remi found the rusted thing, and opened it immediately, pushing my inconsolable self-first before jumping in himself.

I could not imagine what my mother would go through upon seeing my father's dead body on the doorstep. My cowardice was the sole reason for this. I may have been able to save my father, but I couldn't do it in the face of an adversary such as Remi. A man who did not hold any regard for human life.

"Why did you kill my fucking father Remi" I said, as I cleared my eyes from the tears I had shed. "He can still live, I need to call a hospital". I grabbed my phone, but Remi smacked it out of my hand immediately.

"He was a loose end. You don't understand Ricardo. We couldn't keep him alive." He finally managed to start the car, as I looked around, hoping someone had noticed the commotion that occurred at our doorstep.

The feeling was indescribable. My heart felt like an anvil that had been dropped from a high summit.

Remi finally got the car moving and started driving away from the neighbourhood. At this point, I was praying and hoping the police were on our tail, as I would rather rot in a cell than stay in a car with a psychopathic killer. The way the bullet pierced my father's skin kept replaying in my head, as I struggled for air. Was I ever going to see my mother again?

Remi kept on driving to seemingly nowhere, as I tried to console myself. I was in a car with a senseless killer, who had no morals and no regard for who he was with. I knew that it was a real possibility that I was simply another 'loose end', and he wouldn't hesitate to kill me in a heartbeat if I did anything out of order. I continued to try and control my breathing as I kept recounting my father's death.

Remi, with bloodstains still visible in his hands, stopped again at the apartment, and went inside for a couple minutes.

I quickly reached for my phone in a fit of panic and dialled 911. All that was left was to press the call button, but I couldn't bring myself to do it. My mind constantly told me to do it, but I knew that the police would see me as no more than an aid to a senseless killer. I could have stopped him. My cowardice was the sole reason my father is now dead. Those days in which he would call me a failure made me wish for his death, but now it has happened, and I could not feel more regretful of my actions.

Remi arrived again, and I quickly hid my phone to avoid suspicion. After all, I was also a recluse along with him.

He came out with the prostitute's body, and quickly stuffed it inside the car.

He looked around for one second to see if anyone had saw him. I held out hope that somebody had. It was around 4 in the morning, and I only dreaded to think what was next in this deviant, tumultuous journey. He sat back down in the driver's seat, and for once, calmy said – "Ricardo, we need to go to Vegas."

DEATH

I woke up from my hell. This was a hell unknown to me, a new type of torture that I had now been exposed to. I must have passed out from the constant wailing I had done throughout the trip. I opened my eyes to see the truck at the side of the highway, and Remi outside, smoking a cigarette. We stopped at what looked like a deserted wasteland. The hills that stretched far beyond the horizon, and the washed-out colour of the burned floor. And to my right, the sight of cars zooming past at lightning speeds, with our truck slightly raised onto the desert.

I felt a sense of numbness as I sat there, soaking in my own bodily fluids on the fabric seat. I could feel the heat from the second I opened my eyes, as the yellow haze throughout the desert reflected onto the car.

I didn't want to wake, as I had hoped what had happened last night was simply a nightmare. But this was worse. The pungent smell of the dead body at the back permeated throughout the car as I held my nose immediately.

I needed to come to terms with the fact that my father had died. But it was my mother's reaction to his death that prompted my melancholy. Could I even see her again? I was now 'on the run', for lack of a better word.

Remi quickly stomped on his cigarette and walked toward the car. His face only reminded me of the horrors he had committed, with the dried blood still visible on his hands. Every time I saw Remi, I could not envision anything other than sheer terror. He opened the door and sat inside the truck once more.

"Fuck, that shit smells bad" he said. He must have caught the wafting smell of the dead woman in our trunk. He covered his nose, and got out once more.

"Ricardo, get out of the car" he said. It sounded more like an order rather than a gesture, so I decided to follow through. We both gawked at the trunk, with the smell getting ten times worse upon getting closer.

"Come, let's dispose of it" he said.

I panicked. I took one more glance at the vast desert wasteland and saw no feasible place to hide this suitcase. There were bushes scattered around, but no place to hide a body in a discreet manner.

"Where should we dispose it then?" I replied. I pointed toward the stretches of desert, as if I were inviting him.

"It can't stay there. I can't fucking drive with that smell in the back. We need to dispose of that shit right now." Seems like Remi knew I was being sarcastic. "There is definitely somewhere here to chuck this shit", he said as he signalled for me to get into the car. He closed the trunk and got inside.

He grabbed the phone holder clip from the dashboard, and put it over his nose, and fired up the truck.

Suddenly, he swerved the car, brushing past the barbed wire fence along the side of the highway and so we began to search for a place to put the body. He was right about the smell however, as it dominated cabin. We eventually found a couple of crooked standing trees, with branches that could most likely hide the suitcase. Remi parked the truck amongst the trees and quickly got out. He turned the back of the truck to the trees, so people would not discover the heinous act we were committing. I clenched my fists as he opened the trunk and instructed me to help him. I reluctantly got out of the passenger seat and viewed the body once more. The smell was the least of my worries in that moment.

"Okay, when I say lift, we pick the body up and put it in that tree crevice there" he said. It was a rather discreet crevice, with spiky branches overlapping the centre.

"Alright, lift" he said. I picked it up, but to no avail. I dropped the body on the sand, as it was heavier than I had initially anticipated.

"You fucking idiot, grab the fucking thing again" he said, whilst his face was in his palms.

I obliged, whilst my heart was still racing. I tried with all my might, and just about managed to throw the body onto the crevice.

I knew that if someone picked up the smell we would be finished, but I only wanted safety from Remi. Flies quickly swarmed the suitcase, trying to unravel what was trapped below.

I couldn't bear to open the suitcase, as did Remi. I had seen dead bodies before, but this was a whole new world of discovery.

"What about her family" I said, in a melancholic tone.

Remi chuckled a bit and cleared his throat.

"Ricardo once again, she was a fucking whore. I doubt she even cares about her family, just like how she didn't care about her shitty job." He wasn't even drunk this time, in which I would simply cite it as irrational drunken thought. This was his rational state. "Now, are we going to sulk over this bitch or are we going to move it". I obliged, as we walked away from the body. I observed it one more time, to check if it was properly hidden.

The suitcase was out of sight, but that killing would not be out of mind for a while.

We sat in the car for a while, until I heard a vibration. It was my phone. I saw the caller, my mother. Initially, I was met with grief as well as joy, as I needed to answer as I knew she probably had discovered my father's body.

Suddenly, as I rushed to answer, Remi knocked the phone out of my hand as it crashed onto the car's floor.

"Don't fucking answer it." He said, whilst also grabbing his gun to make sure I was kept in check. "Fuck, fuck fuck" he told me, whilst having his hands in his face. "The police are going to fucking track that thing". He quickly grabbed the phone from the floor, as my mind urged me to snatch it out of his hand. Yet, his gun was on full show, pointing directly at my skull.

"Fucking stay there" he said, whilst emitting his heavy breathing. He kept the gun locked on me as I started to feel tightness in my lungs. I needed to answer that call. My mother. My mother. I tried to control the breathing, but I couldn't. I felt like dying of asphyxiation right then and there.

Remi came back to the car and immediately started it. I now had no way to contact my mother, and no way to tell her I was innocent.

My life had now slowly started to descend into tragedy. Surely now I was a prime suspect. We sped off on the highway, near Fresno and intended to never look back. At least, that's what Remi said. I had a strong feeling that the search was being conducted for the prostitute we just disposed of. And I knew that she would be relatively easy to find, judging by the smell.

"We need to fuck off from here quick" he said, as he sped up.

"They're going to track that fucking phone, I just know it", he continued to say as he changed lanes in a matter of seconds. Despite not hearing much, I knew that the police were on our tail.

We continued down the stretches of deserted land for hours until Remi decided to slow down and stop.

"Fucking hell" he said as he slowed down. It seemed even he was tired of driving, after boasting about being on the run.

"How do you work the radio on this thing?" he said, as he messed around with the buttons himself.

I quickly showed him how it worked, and soon enough, I realised that my biggest fear had somehow come true. I didn't listen to large parts of it, but one part I did clearly identify.

"The police have now identified the prime suspect as 23-year-old Ricardo Joaquin Castillo, in the murder of his father"

There was no mention of Remi. I listened for a couple minutes more, yet no sign of him also being one of the suspects.

I started breathing heavily once more. My phone had been destroyed, I was in a car with a murderer, and the police supposedly have no evidence for him being involved. I was the only one being named.

"How the fuck has this happened" I said as I continued to breathe heavily, almost fainting once more.

"Listen Ricardo. Don't fucking panic now. We are going to a safe place, where you can stay until this all blows over". He put his thick arm around my back. For a moment, I forgot that this was the man who brought about these feelings of melancholy and dread. But in that moment, I needed to trust him. Or else, my entire liberty would be jeopardised.

"Listen, you don't need to trust me. Just know that if you get caught, I get caught aswell. And I will be charged for much deeper shit" he said, as he fired up the truck again. We still had around 5 hours before we could reach Vegas, and I could only hope and pray that the police didn't catch our trail too soon, for I would be in much graver trouble.

As the car moved through the seemingly endless freeway once more, I would periodically look back to make sure that nobody had emerged behind us.

"Fuck" Remi said, out of the blue.

"I'm hoping I destroyed that phone, or else the police will find that whore's body"

He continued down the straight road, with one hand being curled up in a fist. I continued waiting, as I wanted to end my life right there and then. After all, I felt my whole life crash right in front of me. It was too late to go back and retrieve the body.

Remi turned the radio off and continued speeding through. We had now made it to sunset. We were running low on gas, and intended to stop by a gas station before we continued. I hoped we wouldn't stop for a while, as I was getting increasingly paranoid of the police being on our heels.

I knew we had to stop, hence I allowed it. Not that my input mattered in the situation anyways. I knew that my mother would never talk to me again after this, as I assumed she had developed some levels of hatred for me, thinking I was the one who killed my stepfather. Yet, I was also being held at gunpoint. The worst of all, the killing was highly believable as I had publicly shown my mother the hate I held for him after being kicked out. It turns out I truly did not dislike him, but my screams and cowardly actions were not enough. I knew that I cannot be forgiven for staying still and watching at it is something I will hold in my sullen heart for a long time.

We stopped at a nearby gas station, and Remi grabbed the wad of cash he threw over the prostitute's dead body.

"Also, we aren't making any fucking card payments. It's too risky" he said. It seemed like he knew how this deviance worked. His calmness only brought me more sorrow, as I knew he was subconsciously teaming with happiness inside as he wasn't framed for a heinous crime.

"Keep your head down, don't let anyone view you", he said as he entered the gas station. I agreed, and got down. Several thoughts had already entered my head throughout the trip. Many of these thoughts told me to find a way to commit suicide, and that wasn't far from what I was intending. Was it better than sitting in a car with a killer? I had no family to nurture me, nor did I have any proper 'friends'. The one 'friend' I had has now turned my life into a living hell. I swallowed my last ounces of pride, and curled up in the passenger seat, I made the decision to kill myself.

THE WORLD'S REVENGE

REMI PALLUDAN, 19 JULY 2009

I loved the act of killing. The feeling of power it would provide me was second to none. I grabbed the gun and shot it right through the whore I had just fucked. It was quicker than I had anticipated, simple. All that was needed was a quick blast to the whore's head. She screamed for a bit, but the job was done. Her blood was laid all across the floor, whilst I quickly hammered her flip phone, whilst I could only hope she didn't make the decision to call the police.

I bent over to see her dead body. Surprisingly, I held no remorse for what I did. My only concern was my 'housemates' would make it back and see the crime I had done in this very apartment.

Having used a gun for the first time on another human being, I felt a sense of fulfilment on what I had just done. I stopped her from making that dreaded call to the police and lost my virginity at the same time.

I knew that my time here was over, so I grabbed my packed bag from the other room and tried stuffing her body in it. I removed all her clothes first and grabbed her thighs I had just indulged in earlier, and placed it inside the suitcase. Her body wasn't working with me, as she kept sliding out of the bag. I continued to push her body in further, until I got her in a curled-up position and placed her inside. Now I needed to dispose of her remains. I wanted to burn her body, and that is what I intended to do. I grabbed the suitcase with her body inside of it and took it away. I could hear some banging noises coming from outside, so I went onto her springy box bed, and looked down from the window. They were the usual drunk hooligans, smashing bottles outside the apartment buildings. Most of the tenants who loved here were students anyways, including this bitch before I shot her.

I carried out the suitcase and brought it down the stairs with me. I had dumped some of my things on top of the girl, but only the most valuable items, as I intended never to return to this place. I didn't have any love for this girl, the only thing I intended to do was use her body. I had never thought I would enjoy the act of murder so much that I would impulsively do it. But now, it has happened. The adrenaline rush I had received from shooting the whore was something inconceivable.

Finally using that gun gave me a sense of confidence, and power I had never felt before. I kept moving the suitcase down the staircase, as I looked around and made completely sure that nobody was looking behind me. I was now a killer. I took relish in that title. I always thought that title would give me some form of respect, despite being hated by society. I knew people feared killers, even though they condemned their actions. For that reason, I enjoyed subconsciously calling myself one.

She was no doubt heavy, as I carried on dragging her body down the stairs. My heartbeat started to go up upon seeing those same hooligans from the window. I tried to play it off and walked past them in swift fashion.

The bag gliding across the pavement created a distinct noise as I walked past them, and they looked in my direction for one faint second. I held my breath and knew this could all go haywire if they stopped to question. It was only an innocent bag, after all. I checked my hands in all the commotion, to make sure they were free of any excess blood or something that could incriminate me on the spot. I took one shallow breath and felt the essence of warm air in the summer night as I made it out of the place. I had my key with me and intended to return it for I was not to spend any more time in this place. Vegas was nothing but a nightmare for me, except this very moment, where I felt some form of fulfilment. A twisted fulfilment, but it was one that struck me heavily.

I knew that if I was caught now, I would be on the sex offender's registry for the rest of my mortal life, and rot in jail. I walked through the night, in an incredibly suspicious manner, as I tried to find somewhere I could chuck this girl's body. I longed to do this same deed to Meredith, to see her face in shock and panic as she would be forced to succumb to my wishes. Anyone longs to feel a sense of power over someone who has tarnished your reputation. That didn't matter, however. I needed to place her body someplace she would never be found.

I was clearly struggling to carry this suitcase, as I kept looking for places to end this girl's existence. I knew that people would be looking for her, but I intended to make it out of the state before it got to that point. I wanted to return to Vegas, no doubt, but now was not the time.

I eventually found a place I could properly put her to rest. The long Flowing river all along Peace Waters enabled me to put her body away safely. I looked around, to make sure nobody would look, and wound up putting it away. I knew this saga was far from being over, as I rushed back to the apartment to gather the rest of my belongings. By the time I had reached, I noticed both my 'roommates' were back in the house.

"Lyota, call the police. He's here."

It looked like they were already in mourning. They quickly realised that I was the sole suspect, and as I forgot to clear up some of the blood that had spilled on the hallway, I was busted. Or so I thought.

The Asian guy came through from Lenora's room. He clearly knew what was going on. "I knew there was something fucked up about you". He said, as my other 'housemate' locked the door.

"You aren't getting out" he said, as he locked it. The Asian guy plucked off his shirt, in a show of dominance as he tried to pin me down.

We tousled for a bit, as he failed to bring me down. I eventually took hold and pushed him into the wall. I knew exactly what needed to be done. I needed to kill both immediately. I had already been desensitized to killing, so I knew this would be easy.

"Where the fuck is she" my other roommate said, as he started crying as he said it.

They immediately set off after me as I rushed to grab my gun. There it was, in all its glory on the wooden desk in my shanty room. I didn't think twice as I pulled back the safety. Eventually they bust inside the room and attempted to bring me down. They did, and I felt the weight of two gym rats immediately. Their bodies were sweaty as I could feel them trying to strangle and kill me.

I hoped they couldn't see the gun as I was struggling for air.

"Where did you put her body you fat shit" one of them said, as I made erratic noises to try and escape this predicament.

"don't tell me you fucking killed her"

I knew the answer, I felt like saying it, but I needed to shoot him first. I was gasping for air, as I couldn't hold on any longer. I needed to push, and try and escape, or else I would be the one dying.

I grabbed the hand that was strangling me and pulled it the hardest I had ever done. I needed to escape, I just needed to. I tried to calm myself down before I could wriggle out. I couldn't. I was quickly losing oxygen, as they were dead set on killing me.

"I.. Threw her body in river" I said.

In shock, the Asian fucker broke me free.

"You fucking what?" he said as he signalled for the other guy to call the police.

I knew the safety was off on the gun, as I wasted no time and shot him twice as he signalled. I did the same for the other guy, and through the gunshot, I knocked the phone right out of his hand. I continued to breathe heavily, as I had just escaped the grasp of a strong choke. But they were lying on the floor, the Asian was still conscious.

I laughed at his suffering. His chiselled body, and tough persona all faded away when I heard him screaming for his mother. I felt no remorse as he was groaning in pain and suffering. I laughed, harder than I had ever laughed before. I relished in the fact that I won against a pair of brutes. I enjoyed watching him come to terms with his death.

"Looks like you'll be joining your little friend" I said with a sinister smirk on my face. I had won. He continued to look at the gunshot wound I had inflicted and kept smiling at the sight of it. I had sustained a small wound to my eye, but it was nothing compared to this man who was now going to die.

"What will be your last words?" I said, out of curiosity.

"Please, get my mother" he said, as he struggled to get the words out. His slow passing brought me great joy, but I needed to act quickly before someone came to check on these people. I needed to clean the crime scene and escape back to San Francisco before a police investigation inevitably began.

Lyota died shortly after he uttered those words, and I got to work. I got any supplies I could find in the communal kitchen and grabbed both their bodies. I knew that I could drop them in the river and avoid suspicion, before things started to get even more deranged. I needed to erase any record of my time here, so I checked the gun to make certain that I had enough bullets, as I knew this would not be the last time, I would need to use it.

I found some Windex, and a couple-coloured cloths. The cloths were unopened, so I opened them and decided to spray the Windex on the remnants of blood that were left. I made sure to cover my hands before attempting anything, as I knew the police would be on my tail as soon as I had finished here. The blood was dried up, and I started to scrub it heavily. I did not have great tools to work with, so I decided to make do with spraying the Windex over the blood, in an effort to try and clean the blood as fast as I could. I didn't feel stressed, but this was one of those times. I dragged both men's corpses down the hallway and bundled them up together. I didn't have another bag, as I had used it to dump the other bitch down the river. My impulsive decision to kill was feeling more like a problem every single second I looked at those bodies.

I rubbed my eyes for a bit, just to assess the situation, and began to look around for something to put their bodies in. Both of their rooms were locked, so I grabbed the keys they each had on their person and unlocked one of the doors. I rummaged around in both rooms, trying to find something to put their bodies inside. I found trash bags, but nothing more than rucksacks in the closet. I grabbed those to put my belongings in, as I had dropped my suitcase in the river.

I continued to pace up and down the house, unsure of what to do to these bodies.

I was erratic, and decided against my better judgement, to place the bodies in one room, and bolt the door shut. I had moved them around three times now, and needed somewhere where they could rot in peace. I could already sense that the bodies were beginning to decompose. I needed to place them somewhere that could mask the smell and raise little suspicion.

Could anyone hear the gunshots I had just fired?

I placed the bodies on top of each other inside the closet. I lined the closet with all the blankets from the house, and the thickest spare duvets I could find. After placing those bodies inside, I wrapped it in the thick wad of blankets and linen, and forcefully shut the closet door. I could not think of such a thing right now. I took a deep breath before deciding to search the room for any valuables. I needed to take something tangible to ensure my survival. I began emptying the closets and drawers from all my housemates, and amongst all the childhood photos and pictures of their parents, I found some great shit. I managed to gather 2 seemingly gold watches and a couple gold bracelets and necklaces. Most of them were from Lenora's room, and I had to rummage through multiple photos and trinkets in order to get what I really wanted. I placed them in the rucksack I had stolen, alongside my other belongings.

The whole house was a mess from top to bottom. I knew I had a day at max to get myself out of the state before something bad was going to happen. Rent was also due tomorrow, and by now my parents were not going to pay for it. I made sure my room was completely empty, and just how it had been left, so that no one had suspected I had moved in.

But I needed to enact another plan that would maybe involve another killing. I needed to avoid that rent payment at all costs. And that meant for all of us.

I set the jewels down and went back into the cupboard and grabbed the two bodies. I rummaged around in their pants to find some form of ID, and I got some. Two drivers' licences with their full names on both. I rushed into Lenora's room to grab any Id I could find, and I did through an old concert ticket, with her full name on it.

It was a fucking Britney Spears concert. Just seeing that made me content that I killed her.

I now knew what their names were, and I decided to leave. I knew the reception was open for 24 hours, and I intended to make sure we were all wiped off the system. When I entered the place with my father, I realised they had all the names of the tenants on a computer log, and I needed them to erase all record, before the next receptionist took charge at 6am. I made haste and proceeded to leave the place and to shut the cupboard, replacing the lining I had installed. I knew it may have not been enough to mask any smell, but I knew it bought me time, something I had very little of. I quickly grabbed a pink cloth from Lenora's room, and some sunglasses I had found in the communal kitchen. I put the sunglasses on immediately, as I rushed downstairs and locked the door. There was a little window, so I could see what was happening at the reception desk before I made any brash decisions. A short, brunette lady was sitting down, half asleep with a pamphlet of some sort masking her eyes. As far as I was aware, there was nobody else there, so I needed to make my move, quickly.

I swallowed my breath, and looked around, and that's when I disabled the safety on my gun and went in. There was a small, rusted bell on the desk itself and I proceeded to press it harshly, almost blowing the pamphlet off the lady's eyes. She was much more attractive with the leaflet on her face, but I had no time to debate that. I completely forgot to think about what I was going to say to her in order to get her to erase my name off the tenants list, and I trembled.

"Can I help you?" she said. She had a very obnoxious voice. Couple that with her abnormally proportioned face, she didn't exactly light any fireworks in my mind.

"Ah, yes I just want to pay my rent, as I know it's due"

"And your name is?"

"Remi. Remi Palludan" I said, whilst I kept the gun in my pocket, holding it still.

"Lemme just find your name on here" she said as I waited to strike. I knew it would only be a matter of seconds, but I needed her to do some tasks for me.

 "Alright, are you going to pay it here, or via cheque?"

I smiled. "I'll pay all of it here". I needed to do it. Now. Right fucking now.

I lost control, as I pulled my gun out and pointed it straight at her face, whilst putting the cloth on my face.

"Alright, here's what I want you to do. I need you to erase my name from your fucking records. Do it. Now."

She was shocked and put her hands up in fear. I had never struck such fear in one person before, and despite the complicated circumstances I was in, it felt exhilarating.

"Do it you fucking slut, do it"

I stood behind her whilst keeping the gun pointed at her face. She was sweating, I could feel it.

"Please, don't hurt me. I have a family. My son's in the first gra-"

 "I don't give a fucking shit about your son. Do as I say bitch" it felt pleasuring, just to get those words out against a woman. I wished to do the same to Meredith, if I ever saw that whore again.

I watched as she clicked on my name and couldn't find anything to erase my existence. Something told me that she genuinely did not Know what she should do, but another part told me that she was just buying time for someone to come and arrest me. I knew I could kill.

She had a family, however. My moral dilemma subsided as she tried to run out. She was going to rat me out, so I wasted no time and shot her in the back before she could make a break for it. I fired two shots and dragged her body back onto the stool she was sitting on and placed a pamphlet on her face. The heavy breathing continued as I place my gun down and tried to work my head around this computer. The endless amounts of time I would spend chronically online, I felt that I was qualified enough to erase myself off this pay system. I clicked on my name amongst the hundreds of names once more and viewed the details. I scrolled for a couple seconds before I could hear speaking outside. I needed to wrap this up quick. My breathing intensified once more as I vigorously scrolled with the mouse to view all the options.

One option finally stood out, which said, 'remove user data' and I clicked on it feverishly. I knew that I needed to do the same for the other two people I had killed.

I had developed a knack for killing, as I had done it three times in one night. Endless amounts of sweat trickled down as I tried to remember the names of whom I had killed. I looked outside to see a watchguard approaching, slowly. Fuck. My adrenaline skyrocketed as I maintained a glare on the guard with the corner of my eye. I eventually found the Asian guy, Lenora, and the surfer guy, and managed to erase their names on the system. I needed to get out of the place before things got ugly, and if the watchguard saw what I was doing. I wrapped it up and grabbed the woman's body. Should the police enter the place, they will find no records of my existence.

I made haste and left the building, with nothing left for me to do. It was almost 6am, and with a heavy lack of sleep, I needed to escape. With my gun. I love murder.

WANTED

"The police have now issued an arrest warrant for the suspected killer of Carlos Joaquin Castillo, his son Ricardo Joaquin Castillo. Police suspect that Castillo has left the state of San Francisco as evidenced by the missing truck he is thought to have stolen. San Francisco Chief of police, Mr Derek Choi has ordered a citywide manhunt of the individual, whilst police will travel state lines in order to track the stolen truck in an effort to find Ricardo, and hopefully arrest this senile kil-"

"Fuck." Remi said as he turned the radio off.

I chuckled a little as he said that.

"You aren't the one being searched for, Remi. You ruined my fucking life, and now you're the one fucking worrying? My father is fucking dead, I don't have a goddamn fucking phone, and my mother is inconsolable because she thinks her only son killed him, that's worthy of the word 'fuck'." Remi looked at me, with a serious stare as if he were listening to me. He never listened. He never will. I knew this fucker very well at this point. "My fucking life has been ruined; you know that?" I continued to say. I wanted to speak my mind to this immoral recluse as I didn't care whether he decided to pull the trigger on his treasured gun or not.

"The police are fucking looking for me, they have started a manhunt. I'm dead meat." I said.

Remi looked back. For once, he would feel a sense of guilt. Something he rarely would do.

"Ricardo. We will get out of this. It's dangerous for me to go back to Vegas, but since the police have started a hunt, I'm risking my own fucking safety to ensure yours, so maybe shut the fuck up a little before I blast a bullet down your fucking head." He said, as he grabbed his gun from the cupholder.

I couldn't care less that he was threatening me. His threats meant seldom to me anyways. I had made the decision to kill myself, and I would stick with it. I had nothing to live for. My chances for a normal life were now certainly ruined at the hands of this conman.

"Do it. Shoot me in the fucking face Remi. I dare you"

I wanted to ease myself to death, and I would achieve that by any means necessary.

"Let's just leave" Remi said, as he started the car again. I knew now that deep down he did not want to murder me, as he had done with multiple people before. I knew that I needed to escape, and he would not stop me.

"We need to find somewhere to stay, anyways. We are fucking bedraggled" he said, in a softer voice than previously.

I could agree with that, I was in desperate need of a shower, and some clean clothes. But with a nationwide search to my name, I needed to act in a different manner.

We found a motel a couple miles away and set off in the truck. We both knew this wouldn't last long, as the police were most likely looking for the exact truck as we were driving through the freeway with it.

I didn't usually pray. But in this moment, I needed some form of divine intervention to pull me out of this situation. We sped off into a shanty motel a couple miles off the freeway. It looked like something straight out of a Wild West movie. We pulled into the parking lot, and Remi instructed me to get down. I did, and he went inside. I waited for about 20 minutes in the scorching car, hearing buzzards scream above me with endless amounts of cacti scattered along the deserted wasteland. The parking lot was covered in the sand dust, with the wind pushing it along.

Remi came back from the inside, and instructed me to come in. I felt naked as I stepped out of the car. My whole body felt sticky, as the fabric on my clothes clung onto my person. I needed a shower, badly. I wasted no time in getting out of that frying pan, and into the room, in the most discreet manner I had ever done.

The room was nothing to write home about, the dust was everywhere, with the room mats blackened with cigarette burns all over them. Not to mention the wafting cigarette smell that emanated as soon as I stepped foot inside the room. There was no better place for me to stay anyways, so I obliged and turned on the rusted fan in the corner of the room.

"I'm going to make a call" Remi said. "Why don't you hop into the shower". I decided against all good calls, that I would go and shower, since I could physically feel my clothes cave into my torso. I assumed Remi made an important call, something that would maybe give us the slightest bit of safety.

I entered the bathroom, and it was arguably even worse than the main room. The cigarette smell wafted into this room, and it was even worse here. I turned on the showerhead, and I wasn't surprised to see the water pressure low, and cold. I needed a shower anyways, so I decided to take of my clothes, regardless. I observed my body once more, the folds of my skin had lessened. The plump round face I once had was still there, but you could see the weight I had shredded. For once I felt an odd sense of confidence about my smaller size. But what use was it, when the police are on a search for you. I entered the running shower; the water hadn't got any better. I gave it muckle care as I began to use it. It was ice cold, but it felt nice after being soaked up by the desolate heat in the desert. The pure smell of running water didn't mesh well with the smell of cigarette smoke. I ran my fingers through my wet hair. They were almost crying out for some form of cleanliness, as I cascaded through them.

The shower was a form of temporary pleasure. A form of escape from the harsh punishment I was about to be subject to if I were to get caught. I never trusted Remi; he never was a 'friend'. Despite my drop in weight, I still wanted to commit suicide. I had nothing to live for, yet everything to lose.

I got out of the shower to hear a knock on the motel door. I quickly retreated inside the bathroom as Remi opened the door. For all I knew, it could be the police here to arrest me.

Remi opened the door, it was a woman, dressed in scantily clad clothing. Was it another prostitute?

"Remi, you can't keep ordering prostitutes to our door" I said.

"It helps me relieve fucking stress" he said back.

This only increased my desire to escape from his grasp.

"How much for an hour?" he asked.

The woman, who looked like a certified druggie, looked back at him, with her drug-stained eyes.

"100 bucks for an hour" she said.

Even I knew that was shocking, having only been with one prostitute. It baffled me however, how calm Remi was about the fact that I was soon to be arrested.

"Fuck me then" Remi said, as he signalled for her to come closer. I would not bear one second with this tramp, as she looked like she had been taking the pills for a while.

I decided to wear some fresh clothes and sat down doing nothing whilst Remi went to town on this whore. I'm sure he was not wearing a condom, either. His all too familiar heavy breathing began to occur, as I couldn't stand the sight of him.

He finished much sooner than I had initially thought, and actually paid the money this time. Quite rare for someone like him to do.

"I need some fucking booze" he said. I was heavily reluctant to tell him to get some, but I needed some in the moment as much as him. The room service telephone was right next to him, but since he had just been fucked, he needed to clean up.

I decided to pick up the phone and order some beverages. Judging by the quality of the room, I didn't expect the room service to be something extravagant.

"Fuck, I'm going to have a shower" Remi said, as he went into the bathroom. I knew this was a good time to escape, but I couldn't do it. I would think my survival relied on the fact that Remi knew how to get us out of this, but his attitude thus far, had told me otherwise. I could leave, go straight to the police and turn myself in. But I knew I wouldn't have the courage to do that. I could be reunited with my mother, but then I would be convicted of a crime I did not do. Remi needed to be sentenced, or else I would be found guilty. Fuck. I needed to do something, fast. I couldn't. Besides, how would I find my way back in the middle of a deserted freeway? It was an irrational decision.

Soon enough, there was a knock on our door. After the news that I was a suspected killer, I felt reluctant and scared to open doors. I took a breath, as I knew this was most likely the room service.

"Your drinks, sir" a short, plump man said as he handed two cheap bottles of vodka, along with some paper cups.

"Thanks" I said, as I tried to mask my identity as much as possible. I set the drinks down on the table, waiting to consume them.

I cracked open a bottle immediately, as I was just waiting to let loose and drink my pains away. It had been a long while since I had drunk any alcohol, and I needed it, before I went insane in Remi's company.

I needed to find help. Would my mother even acknowledge me as her son after what had happened?

I longed to find my mother, and tell her that this was not me, and that I needed her, desperately. For my fate is now in the hands of a psychopath.

I didn't have a phone either, so contacting my parents was off the radar as well. I took a sip of this cheap vodka, as it stung me right in the throat. It was bitter beyond belief, and it did not have that distinctive taste that all vodka should have. I should have known that this motel wasn't the finest quality, judging from the pungent cigarette smell. Arguably, it was even worse than that whore we killed.

Remi came out of the shower, soaking wet. His folds were worse than mine. His fat was off the charts, as I had never seen him half naked.

"Ah, the booze is here" he said. Remi being drunk is a state I now know, is extremely hazardous. I needed to make sure he did not get too drunk, as his sanity levels fluctuated even worse than my deceased stepfather.

"Don't drink it too much."

"I won't. Don't you want some? Relax a little" he said, as he was already pouring himself a glass.

"I already had some." He nodded as he downed the cheap vodka like it was nothing.

"Remi, my family is gone now. Thanks to you. I'm contemplating killing myself, because of what you did. My life has been ruined, yet you get whores to our room, and get a quick fuck whilst I'm here debating whether or not I am going to live the next day or not."

Remi kept drinking, but he listened to what I had to say.

"Ricardo, I'm fucking stressed out. Who's the one driving you to safety? Me. Who's the one who is risking their life and not just dumping your ass on the street? Me."

I was confused at his face for a second.

"Why the hell are you going to Vegas anyways? I thought you said you would never go" I said to him.

"That fucking whore. She's there. Fucking Meredith." He put his cup down as he took a deep breath.

"The girl from the picture?" I still had it, in my suitcase. She was a beautiful woman, that's all I could infer from it.

"Yes, it's that girl". He spoke. He now got comfortable in his seat and placed the plastic cup down. "I was trying to erase names off a database in my house there, and that's when I saw her fucking name on the list. Meredith Catherine Brown. I knew that one day I needed to find her and kill her as my final act." He spoke. "I also saw where that bitch worked. 'The Honey's Strip club' in Vegas. That fucking whore."

I froze in my seat, as he said those words. His intention was to murder more people, and the girl in the photo was his main target. 'Meredith'.

"How do you know she's still in Vegas?" I said as I looked at him. He had closed the vodka bottle now and put the cup in the small trash bin next to his bed.

"We don't know. But it's my best bet. All the fucking sluts go to fucking Vegas." He said. "If I get arrested, I only want it to be for killing that fucking bitch"

I pulled out the photo I kept of this 'Meredith'. She looked no older than twenty-five in that image. I showed it to him, as he grabbed it and ripped it up.

"I need to fucking kill her" he said.

It didn't feel real, the fact that I was sitting in a motel room with someone who had intentions to kill and inflict harm onto another person. A couple months ago, I was playing mah-jong in the college library, but now my whole life has been turned on its head. I still had ambitions to escape and commit suicide. That was the only way I could escape this hell, that Remi Palludan has created for me. Dusk swiftly arrived, I could see it through our blurred, grimy 'window', with cigarette butts scattered along the windowsill. I guess this was my first night on the road. I don't think I can even sleep anymore, as placing my eyes closed would only bring me the perceived sight of my hysterical mother, and the prostitute we had slaughtered and whacked on the side of the road. I made the chilling assumption that her family would pinpoint me as the sole suspect. Nothing filled me with more disgust than the sight of Remi Palludan.

"Ricardo, we will get out of this, don't worry. You will, anyways" He spoke. "This whore, Meredith has plagued my mind for 10 years. I need to end my suffering. And it will come when I slaughter her." He was dead set on killing Meredith.

"Why the fuck do you hate her so much?" I spoke. This was my question from the beginning. The reason as to why she was ingrained in his mind more than the two people he had killed in front of me. He got up, and I moved back, as I thought he would do something. But no. He reached for his rucksack. A rucksack which had multiple rounds of bullets inside of it. I braced myself for what he was going to pull out. It was a diary like notebook, with a ripped-out piece of lined paper displaying the title.

It said – 'The World's Revenge'.

"Read that and give it back to me in the morning. I doubt you'll get much sleep anyways." He said, as he got prepared for slumber himself. He was probably right. I myself knew that I wouldn't get a wink of sleep. Even thinking about sleep would bring me back the thoughts of my mother, who has now most likely turned on me. The room stank of cigarettes, which heavily clogged my nostrils as I opened this book. It was a diary, which probably contained some fucked-up shit as evidenced by the title. It was now the dead of night, as I refused to go to sleep. Remi however, his peaceful sleep only made me want to shoot him in the dead of night. If only I could find his gun, maybe I would be able to.

There was no point in shooting him. It would only bring me more difficulty. He wasn't a suspect, after all.

His diary shocked me. It also showed me that this wasn't the first time he had killed people before. He had done it to multiple innocents, with no regard for their lives, or families. He truly was a psychopathic killer, one who would stop at nothing to get what he wanted.

I now knew that I was an intermediary in Remi's quest to kill this, Meredith. I was a mere bystander. He used me; in ways I could not conceive.

We were in the Endgame now.

THE LONG HAUL

"The police search continues for 23-year-old Ricardo Joaquin Castillo, and police now suspect he has committed two murders, after tracking Castillo's cellular device. Police say they have found the body of Florence Jimenez, a prostitute who operated around the sketchy 'Tenderloin' district. Her body was found naked, in a suitcase a couple metres away from Castillo's phone, which was also found shattered along the California I-5 freeway. Jimenez was declared missing a couple days ago, but police have now confirmed the body was indeed Florence Jimenez. The search for Castillo is now nationwide, as the San Francisco Police Department fears another serial killer may be on the loose."

Fuck. I should have jumped off the roof when I had the chance. I fell asleep for a couple hours, but I could not stop thinking about the fact that I was named, and a photo was released of me to the news. There really is no escape from my eventual arrest, other than me killing myself.

Remi eventually woke up and we needed to leave. He wasn't asleep when I turned on the news, and certainly wasn't shocked to see my face on there.

"We need to abandon that truck" he said, in a groggy morning voice. It was midday, and we needed to set off immediately, as the police were most certainly on our trail now that they discovered the body, we left 3 hours away.

"The police are closing in on us, Remi" I said, as I immediately got my things and went for the door. We need to leave, quickly."

He got himself out of bed and got ready. I handed back his diary before I could see it any further.

"It was eye opening" I said, as I gave the diary back. You clearly have experience. I had so many questions I needed to ask, but I held them back if it made him get ready faster.

"We are leaving the truck" he said whilst he whacked on a shirt.

"Then what are we driving?" I spoke.

"It's too dangerous to drive it, if the police are on our tail. We'll need to adopt a better approach".

I didn't know what we needed to do, but if it involved killing, I had no choice but to run away.

"Let's just get out of here" I said, as I made my way for the door.

"Ricardo, we are going to get caught if we are seen outside with that thing. We need something else"

I needed to trust him, unfortunately. There was no way I would be on the run for this long if it weren't for him.

Remi got ready and placed his diary in the bag. He grabbed his gun and loaded it. I knew that he needed to kill someone. But who? He signalled for me to get out and we went down to the front.

My heart started pounding as Remi went to the reception desk. Sitting there was a rather plump, Mexican looking individual, with a gravy stain on his bright red shirt. I stood near the stairs, just in case something was to happen.

"You here to return your keys?" he said.

"Well, yes but I also need something." Remi replied.

"At your service, sir" the plump Mexican said to him.

"Where's your car?" he said back.

"Why would you need my car sir?" my teeth chattered as I knew this may be another murder site, which would certainly lead the police to our location.

"Give me the fucking car, or you will die" he said, as he now pointed his gun at him. There were no other workers in the motel, Remi probably knew that.

The motel worker immediately handed his keys as he kept repeating 'don't shoot' about a dozen times.

I couldn't comprehend what Remi's though process was in this moment, if he was going to kill him or not. He didn't. And signalled me to come. I came forth, and he threw his keys to me.

"What's the registration number bitch" he said, as he kept his gun locked on him.

"057 892" he said, as Remi stayed with him.

"Ricardo, grab the bags and come out front, I won't be long". I knew he was going to die. There was no other option. I ran outside with the bags and searched for the licence plate the man had given us. It was a rusted Ford Fiesta, with the red paint chipping off. In all my years of life, I had never driven a car before, so this was going to be the first time. I had never even attempted to, but I needed to now. I opened the trunk and placed my belongings there before I ran to the front seat and started the car up. I could just speed away, and leave Remi for dead, but I couldn't drive.

I started the car and held my breath as I pressed onto the gas. I moved at a steady pace and pulled up front of the reception. Suddenly Remi ran from outside and signalled for me to jump into the passenger side. He threw his rucksack inside and immediately got going once he managed to get in.

"Fuck" he said as he went at speeds that I had never experienced in my life.

"What happened back there" I said, as he continued to push the accelerator vigorously.

"Someone was back there and called the fucking cops" he spoke as I froze in my seat. "They're going to find you if we don't fucking speed past here"

I took a glance at the dashboard. He was driving at the speed of 100 miles per hour. He kept switching lanes, as the other cars stared at us, and I tried to cover my face as he did.

"Fuck, fuck get in the back" Remi said.

"Why?"

"Just fucking do it don't ask questions"

I hastily unfastened my seatbelt and jumped into the back. It was no easy task, however. My body would not fit properly. I bruised my nose as I fell into the black leather seat, hiding my face as Remi continued to speed past.

We were en route for the Las Vegas strip, as both of us knew it was easier to blend in with the huge crowds. It was only a matter of time before the police would catch up to us, so we needed to continue driving.

"They're probably looking for the truck" he said. "We have time"
I knew any rational person would tell the police everything, including the fact that we just stole someone's car. I kept my head down as Remi was speeding down the highway, as I felt the shake of the car every time it would move left to right. We were only a couple hours away from reaching the 'City of Deviance' and we weren't going to stop unless it was necessary. I had a long-standing wish to go to Las Vegas, but at a time like this, I could care less about the destination. I was a wanted man, and I felt like I was property. Huddled in the back of a shitty car, being drove by Remi Palludan. I was a couple bucks shy of 1000 dollars, and I knew it was not enough to get me anywhere safe, so as deranged as it was, this man was my best bet.

"It's very possible to lay low in Vegas. You just need to assume a fake identity and run with it" Remi said, as he finally began to slow down the car. I was surprised he didn't crash into anything.

"Did you get the vodka" he said as he continued slowing down on the freeway.

"Yeah sure, let me get it" I grabbed the rucksack he placed his diary in and grabbed the cheap bottle. I was surprised Remi even wanted to drink it. To me, that drink was poison. Bitter, with a rancid taste, when the drink isn't supposed to taste like anything.

Remi grabbed the bottle and downed the bottle quicker than he spent with that prostitute. There was just over half of the drink left, and it was all his. I certainly would not be indulging in it.

Finally, we began to approach some greener areas, after seeing only miles of desert wastelands.

I would find great pleasure in journeying this route without my external dread, but I could not. There was too much on my shoulders to be thinking of even enjoying this trip to the strip. To think that the police were in sight of us was something that made my heart stop every single time I thought about it.

"The police also found out about the other body" I said to Remi.

"I know" he replied. "I should have put your phone somewhere else. It was a mistake. But we are well away from there, we should be able to make it out". Spending this much time in a car with someone would tire anybody out, but it was made worse from the fact that he was a killer. I was feeling uncomfortable in the back, I didn't want anyone to see us, but at the same time my legs were giving in after too long.

"Do you even care that you've killed so many people?" I said. "And what happened to those people Remi?"

Remi smiled as he kept driving. "I just wanted to repay the injustices brought to me in this world. Nothing else." He continued. "I've been exposed to violence for as long as I could remember. It has become, a part of life. I have been brought up around it. Nothing can stop it, not even you"

He was very elusive in the way he spoke. After reading that diary, and staying up most of the night, I sparked a huge sense of curiosity as to what I needed to do.

We were on the road for a couple more hours, and then we needed to find somewhere to stay, in a discreet fashion. Remi's plan was to fake my death and assume a new identity. But it was something I was not ready to do. But at the same time, I needed some way out of this. But my way out was simple. To throw myself off a building in the Las Vegas skyline.

I wanted to kill myself, but I wanted to do it in style. I had amassed a huge following by the police, so I needed to give them, and my family some sort of closure. An end to this madness. And doing that would be the greatest act.

MEREDITH

We had soon arrived in Las Vegas. It was much different than I had anticipated, we arrived just before the night sky came out and the strip would glow in luminescent colours that screamed of deviant acts. I had already dared Remi to shoot me, but assuming a fake identity in order to carry on with my life seemed a long shot. Killing myself was a far-fetched thought, but reading the news reports and manhunts, it seemed like that was closer to becoming a reality, every day. My living hell looked like it was never going to end, even with Mr Palludan arguing otherwise. I watched, as the shows of nudity and endless gambling took hold stronger and stronger as the sun began to set, with the streets being filled with more traffic and deviant men.

The carefree atmosphere of everyone there only strengthened my impression that everyone there was there for pleasure, nothing else. In a fantasy world of casinos and women raining from every single crevice. And I, would be the only one stuck in a rut of depression and devastation. This fantasy was now my refuge.

We were 8 hours away from San Francisco now, and I still felt the eyes of everyone on me. Assuming to be someone I wasn't didn't sound appeasing, far from it.

We parked up a short drive away, at a place called 'Naked City'. It amazed me how wildly different it was to the strip. Deserted and barred off areas, coupled with shotty cable lines and trash oozing out of every single street. Burned walls and graffiti seemed like the norm here, as makeshift cardboard signs acted as notices. We eventually found somewhere next to a shotty Motel 6, and it appeared that we both were a tad bit rattled by what we saw. My heart pounded as I saw the police tape bordering a convenience store just metres away from where we had parked.

"Are you sure this is low-key?" I said, as I pointed at the police tape. We were in the shadow of the radiant strip, as it provided the only lighting to this place.

"It's the only place we can lay low. Less cameras in this area, means that it's harder for the police to track down where we are staying" he said as he turned the shitty car off.

In the face of multi-million-dollar properties, this neighbourhood provided the starkest of contrasts. I felt hesitant to get out of the car, mainly because of the elevated levels of police watching from everywhere.

We offloaded our things at the motel, and Remi wanted to lay low for the night. I sat around for a couple hours, but at that point, I could not do it anymore. Sitting down in hotel rooms which stank of mildew and cigarettes, not being able to sleep for hours on end, and being leashed by a deterministic killer. I needed to escape and make that escape quickly. I had already planned to go atop Caesar's Palace, and jump from there, but I felt like relishing in the deviant night, as I loved to do. The night was where I could find solitude and drown my sorrows. I hadn't eaten in a while, but Remi had taken all my money, including the $1000 I had pocketed. I knew that a night here was expensive, but I went for it anyways. I still had about eighty dollars in my pocket anyways.

I waited until Remi decided to go to sleep and made my move. I grabbed whatever I could, and bolted out of the door, making sure that I had taken every single item with me. Hopefully, this was the last time I saw this deranged mutant as I closed the door in a silent fashion. I took a deep breath, just enough for my lungs to feel depleted of oxygen and made a break for it. I scanned around for an elevator and pressed my hand immediately against the metallic surface. I kept pressing it until I could see those double doors open, scanning to see if I had awoken Remi, or if he was going to shoot me, point blank. I didn't want to die like that, nor did I deserve it. I was ready to go necessary, except for that. I frantically placed myself inside the elevator, my heart making laps as every second passed. The elevator's smell didn't help either. The stained black carpet wafted a smell I could only describe as pungent.

I bolted out of the elevator, covering my face as best I could as I sped past the reception desk. Immediately, I opened the musty double doors to a sea of darkness, with the only beacon being the Las Vegas strip. My primal instincts prompted me to go towards those lights, as I kept running, regardless of what direction I ended up in.

Running surprisingly reignited my hope. I felt like I had been liberated from evil captivity. Obviously now I knew I was on my own, and I was more likely to be captured and locked up. There was a warrant for my arrest, and I did not have a cell phone to communicate with the outside world.

I needed to locate a pay phone and call my mother. That was the first call to action. If she believed me, then I would maybe consider alternatives to ending my life. A life that has been nothing but devastating sorrow and heartbreak, and neglect from my own family. Part of me didn't want to call her. But I knew that if I did, I may have a chance of saving my future. A future that looked more desolate than the desert on the highway. I stopped to catch my breath, as I tried to find a phone to contact my mother. God knows how much distress she would be in. Would she even believe me to begin with? But I needed to do it, it was my only chance of survival. I walked around aimlessly for a bit, trying to find some form of payphone. I finally found one, next to a 7-Eleven just off the road. I quickly grabbed the phone, as I jogged my memory to get my mother's phone number. My heart had never beat this fast if I wanted to call someone, let alone my own mother. But it was the call I needed to make.

I typed the phone number into the keypad and waited patiently for it to ring. God. I hope she was prepared to listen to me. She was the one who started this fiasco anyways. Logical, but flawed.

I heard that familiar phone ring, as my heart started beating even faster.

I was prepared to hang up, as I constantly looked around for anyone who may have notoriously recognised me. And as I was about to put the phone away,

But as I was, I heard the ring stop.

"H-H-Hello?" a frail, crying tone answered. Her words were breaking as she sounded nothing like my mother. But I knew.

I couldn't help but start wailing. I cried like I had never done before. After hearing her voice, it simply just occurred. I couldn't help it. Her life had been ruined, so had mine.

I felt like saying it, my heart began to sink to the point where I could feel it in my throat.

I tried to stop crying, but to no avail. I soon answered.

"Mom, It's Ricardo" I said, dreading what response she would give once I said it.

"P-Please, don't hang up. I need to explain what happened. Please" I tried reasoning with her despite the fact I was crying rivers worth of tears.

"Ricardo, mijo you killed your father. All for a fucking truck?" she said, in broken English.

"I didn't kill him. I really didn't mother, you need to believe me" I said, as I kept looking around the place. "You need to tell the police it wasn't me, it wasn't fucking me" I said, for once trying to bargain with my own mother.

"Mijo, it's too late. The police are searching for you everywhere. And if you didn't kill him, who did?" she said, so naïve in the way she articulated those words.

"Listen, the reason I would go outside a lot was because I was meeting this man who said he could help me find a little joy in my miserable life. But I didn't know he was a deranged psychopath, hell bent on killing women." I said, as I frantically tried to convey the words. "Listen, he killed a prostitute out of rage and used it to leave and escape to another state. And he needed a car, so he killed dad. He wouldn't give it to him. Please, mother. I have escaped, he's going to kill-"I frantically caught my breath as I realised she hung up. Fuck. I was stuck between a rock and a hard place. I wanted to end my life there and then, but I quickly tried to make my way out of there. If anything, calling my own mother made things that much worse. I knew what I needed to do now. I needed to find this 'Meredith'. She may be the only person that may reconcile with the crazy tale of Remi Palludan. After reading that diary, I knew she recognised him well. She would most likely understand that I was the actual one in danger.

I did hear from Remi the other night that she worked at some sort of brothel or 'gentleman's club' in the heart of the strip. I remembered it well. The 'Honey's' club. I had no sense of direction, but I needed to find this place. And quickly. Everything was reliant on the hope of finding Meredith and telling her my dilemma. I had kept her picture that Remi had handed to me, her luscious brunette hair and perfect body proportions only lead me to ponder how she became a whore in the first place. I needed to take Remi's word for it and find this strip club. I tried my best to keep a low profile, but it was late at night, a time where the patrons of bars and strip clubs become black out drunk, pass out and lose memory. Hopefully none would recognise my face. For I was an outcast, a delinquent. I hopelessly looked around for this strip club. There were no signs of it anywhere.

Beyond the hordes of women dressed half naked wandering the barren streets, and the men who were crying on the street having lost hundreds, I looked for that one sign, that one word. I continued searching until it came to a standstill. But beyond that standstill, I looked up, and there it was. The 'Honey's' Gentleman's Club. It looked like the usual tacky, run-down strip club, with the services etched poorly onto the walls, with stock images of women with very little clothing.

I let out a sigh of relief as I finally managed to find the place despite all odds and opened the heavy glass door into the dark club. I saw many women; it was not easy to spot any appearance in that lighting. Money flew in the air like flies, on a slow descent to their death, whilst women acted accordingly, throwing their bodies everywhere for these degenerates. It was a full house, despite the cheap and run down interior. I held onto some hope that I would find 'Meredith' in the crowd, although knowing that she would look very different. I held onto a little shred of hope that she didn't change her appearance that much, after all the picture I saw told me she had a naturally attractive face. But anyone's appearance can change when they are a slut.

I was approached by a rather big and tall man. He was wearing a black polo shirt which blended into the club's setting. He must have been 6'9 or something like that, as his body towered over mine. Making me look even more minute and insignificant to the crowd.

"You here for our services?" he said, looking at me up and down, observing the fact that I probably was the target demographic for a club like this.

"Uh, yeah" I said, nervously. I had no idea how to find Meredith, I had no plan.

He crossed his arms, in typical bouncer fashion. As he did, I could see the word 'SAMOA' tattooed on his arm. He must have been Samoan. The brown skin, and tall stature must have given it away.

"So, you want a private session?" he replied back. As he did, a golden opportunity arose to find Meredith. I needed to find her by booking her.

"Of course, I do" I said, whilst my voice deepened. I needed this. I needed to find Meredith through this one session. I rummaged through my pockets to feel Meredith's picture. I couldn't show it to this Samoan, it would be too suspicious.

"So, how do i get this uh session?" I said, with a hint of suspicion in my voice.

"We have a catalogue." He spoke. "You choose from there". I had never been to a club like this before. I had desires of going to one when I was a virgin, but now my only wish was to find this woman, and hopefully explain to her the predicament I was in. I knew that Remi would be giving chase now, he might know what I would do If I escaped, which I have done.

"Let me see the catalogue then" I said, as he called for someone to get it.

179

"The service is $200. Pay extra if you want to take them home" he said. He was treating the women like objects. They were whores, but no wonder Remi took so much interest in them. They would obey you like a robot. The man came back and handed the Samoan a small menu like leaflet. He passed it to me and waited for my response.

"Take your time" he said. I looked around and glanced at the available girls. They all had names like 'Red' and 'Violet'. Possibly to hide their identities from the men going to the club. I tried to jog my memory and get that picture of Meredith back into my mind, and I matched it with the one named 'Paradise'. She seemed to be the most popular by the looks of things, as her picture was front and centre of the page with the largest photograph. You couldn't miss it.

"I'll take this one" I said, whilst pointing at the picture of Meredith.

"I'll get her ready for you" the Samoan said. He walked away with the catalogue as I quickly pulled out the picture from my pocket. I had no interest in having sex or receiving a 'lap dance'. The only thing I needed as answers, and for someone to listen to me. I knew Meredith would understand the situation, granted Remi's distinct hatred for her. I needed to warn her as well, for Remi had only come to murder her.

The Samoan signalled for me to come, but stopped me at a pink curtain.

"She's behind here. I need payment upfront. She's very popular, so the full service is $220."

Despite very clearly being scammed, I obliged. I only wanted to see Meredith, no matter the price. I knew her looks and aura would be hard to resist but I needed something else from her. She probably doesn't know the situation she is in.

I handed the Samoan the money, as he was gesturing for it constantly. He allowed me to breach the curtain, and upon entering I knew this girl was Meredith. She looked older, more seasoned. But beyond the stripper makeup and feisty look, she was the one I saw in the picture exactly.

"Look at you" she said, in a rather seductive voice. I knew this was all manufactured to uplift a sullen man's fragile ego, they must be paid for it. "So, you want a dance?" she said, as she instructed me to take a seat. She wore a tight black corset, with her legs and cleavage on full display to entice anyone who step foot in this room.

I didn't say 'yes' or agree to anything but paying for the room was enough for her to press her body against mine. She seductively began to remove her clothing, as I took an audible gulp.

"Well, uh listen" I said as she was stripping down.

"Yes?" she said, as she paused for a second.

"You don't need to do all of this" I said as I looked around the private room.

"What do you mean?" as she approached me, with her breasts on full show, stroking my face. I couldn't help but feel a little aroused from the whole ordeal, but I knew what I was about to tell her would shock her to the core.

"Meredith. I need your help."

It seemed like she sprung back into life, and immediately stopped putting on a fake persona. Her eyes widened, as she stepped back from my face.

"Who are you?" she said, in a much more refined and regular voice, as opposed to a sexual, seductive voice.

"Listen. I'm Ricardo. Ricardo Joaquin Castillo. I'm not sure if you read the news, but I'm on the run right now, and I've been framed". I said. I needed to be cautious with my words, as any slip of tongue and I was in police custody.

"Framed for what?" she said, as she was putting the little clothes she had back on.

"Two murders. One of them was my father. I spoke to my mother, to try and clear the air, but I'm pretty sure I only just pinged the police to my location."

She seemed intrigued. This was no longer a conversation that she robotically needed to listen to, this was life or death.

"Who's the actual murderer? And how do you know my name?" Meredith seemed surprised and shocked at the same time. Her face was more innocent when she was intrigued, I could tell.

"It was Remi. Remi Palludan. He needs someone to cover up for eventually killing you, so he brought me to Vegas".

Suddenly, she seemingly froze in her position. She sat down and took a deep breath. Even I would be shocked, and worried if someone like Remi decided to chase me down.

"Meredith, I need you to believe me. Because no one else has" I said. "Otherwise, we both die."

"Where is he now?" she said.

"Most likely outside. Looking for us." I said. "We stayed in a motel, five blocks down, but he's probably noticed the fact that I am gone".

"Does he know that I work here?" she said, seemingly asking me an array of questions to ensure her own safety.

"Yes. That's how I found out" I said. "We probably need to get out of here." I was lucky to have found her before Remi did.

"And this guy had a picture of me?" she said.

"His whole life now is about you. He's a hopeless killer. We can't let him find you"

She seemed petrified in the way I was speaking. Would she even trust someone like me? All I knew was that Remi was lurking, he was going to pounce at some stage, and enter this very strip club. Meredith opened the pink curtain a small bit, just to view what was going on. She looked around, not even knowing what Remi looked like. Maybe the way I described him didn't strike her fancy.

"I can't trust you, Ricardo." She said as she closed the curtain. Despite the horror story I had just explained, I was surprised. But since she was a stripper, I guess she had to be cautious of scenarios like this.

"Listen, this man's only purpose is to find you and kill you. He doesn't even care if he dies himself in the process." I spoke. I needed to convince her; she was my only hope of survival.

"If you choose not to trust me, that's fine, but just know he will not rest until he finds you". I knew she was scared; I was too. But we needed to work together, and I needed her by my side.

"Let's get out of here then" she said. "We'll have to go to my apartment a little early"

"Do I need to pay the extra charge?" I said as I was ready to leave. She looked in confusion, as she opened the pink curtain again. "You're a fugitive. I don't think you need to abide by any laws".

And with that, she left the room, and I was sure to follow her.

I was simply relieved for once, that someone knew that it wasn't me committing these murders. And potentially saving her from the grasp of Remi Palludan. But our time was ticking, in this city of lust and escapism.

THE WORLD'S REVENGE

"The police can now confirm that the search for Ricardo Joaquin Castillo is in its final stages. A phone call traced from the back of a Las Vegas 7-Eleven has now made certain that Castillo had fled to Vegas and enables the police to further strengthen their claim that Castillo was the one who dumped the body of Florence Jimenez off the California I-5 freeway. Police also claim Castillo had an accomplice during these murders, and employees from a motel on the same freeway claim to have been threatened by these two fugitives. The camera caught sight of a man, who authorities say, looks like Castillo in a mask. Police have now said this was done during a trip to Vegas."

The news can be beneficial in some instances. Instances like these. There wasn't long now. I could sense that Meredith was here. Following what I had already knew, and her degenerate face being on the website of the 'Honey's Gentleman Club'. There wasn't long left before the police would eventually find out that I was the one doing the heinous acts that Castillo is being framed for. If I wanted to do something drastic like killing that whore, I needed to do it now. I was going to shoot her on the spot in that club, but after Ricardo's escape act, I could not afford to slip up, anywhere. One brash decision, and I would be the one locked up. I didn't fear going to prison, I feared the fact that I wouldn't fulfil my mind's one desire, which was to eradicate that whore off the face of the earth.

I had no doubt that Ricardo was simply a loose end. I should have killed him when I had the chance. I thought he understood me, he would align with my goal, but for obvious reasons, he did not. I would have no problem in killing him either. If he were to interfere with my one goal. I would think that after reading this, he would understand that everything I was doing was justified, but it was obvious that he tried to break away, and escape. From the looks of things, he doesn't have much time left before he is in police custody. But him being arrested would mean that I would be held accountable for all my misdeeds. After shooting that receptionist, and killing my roommates, they would be able to trace the dots. Not to mention, a couple weeks after I had escaped, the residents of the place began to realise that there were dead bodies, as the smell became overbearing. The investigation proved, muckle care. With no traces of me on the system, they began to assume that one of the housekeepers had killed these people, as they always had free access to the apartments. There was no record of me, I was just a loose end. The thick gloves I wore on that day, masked my fingerprints well. The police swiftly locked off the entire building and interviewed and searched each room thoroughly. Despite their search, their best assumption was the housekeepers who would enter the rooms. They found everything, from knives and guns to other condemnable evidence, but nothing to make them sure I was the one who did these murders. There were no people in that house to testify against me, there was no record I even existed. The housekeepers weren't sufficient evidence after all. The police still had their doubts on who it really was. If Ricardo were to get interrogated by those pigs, he would surely also testify that I killed people in that hellhole.

The investigation is still open, to this day. It is for that very reason I am teaming with agitation and rage after seeing Ricardo escape. There is no way he would mask anything to the police. He is going to ruin everything and get me in serious trouble. From now, my task is simple: Kill that fucking rat before the police gets to him. I needed to put my initial task of killing Meredith on hold, in order to get Ricardo in check. I had to follow police reports, and the news in order to find Ricardo. I knew I should have killed him when I had the chance. Even my heart wouldn't let me kill some people. But that soft spot was no longer there. I would stop at nothing to deviate from my intended

plans. The only problem was being able to find Ricardo before the police did. I had one advantage, however. I knew Ricardo better than the police did. It appeared he had taken the money I had taken off him. The police also had a rough idea of who I was, and that I was allegedly working with Ricardo, but they didn't know that I was the one who committed all these murders. There was no way to contact him, this was partly my fault, as I dumped his phone alongside the body. The news stated that his mother didn't believe him, and that she was the one who informed the police. I knew his mother was not on his side.

I decided to light a cigarette, and smoke. I knew that these pleasures were slowing me down immensely, but I needed to concentrate before I needed to hunt down Ricardo. There were no thrills, just pure hatred and inconvenience. I only brought Ricardo with me to serve as a puppet. I should have killed him when I had the chance. But I couldn't sit here, in this room any longer. The police were going to be all over the state, looking for that fucker. I couldn't rest. I quickly disposed of the cigarette and started rummaging through Ricardo's belongings. I needed to find something that would lead me to him. I found nothing but baggy clothing and old, rusted razors he must have used to shave. I decided these items would be nothing more than fodder, so I quit looking and started searching outside. I needed to use my instincts and predict where he was going to be. The only thing that ran through my head was the possibility that he had killed himself, which seemed like a very rational option. I had somewhat of a feeling that he was growing tired of life, and his family turning against him gave the perfect opportunity to join his father. I ran helplessly onto the skyline and looked around in every direction my body would face. It was a race against time, which I was clearly losing. I knew I needed to stay calm if I really wanted to find him, but there was no way I could. My whole existence could be reversed if the police are to find this rat before I did.

I wandered many bars and looked atop every building to see if he had thrown himself over. Killing himself was the best scenario, for I could peacefully enact my plan, without any interruption. That could be the most likely outcome, but I couldn't stay certain on it.

I carried on circling the bars and nightclubs, squeezing myself through hordes of degenerate waste fodder to catch even a glimpse of someone who looked like Ricardo.

I grabbed a drink and decided to sit. This was the worst solution to my crippling panic, but if it made me calm down just a little bit, I would do it. Staring across the entire strip, it was beginning to simmer down, just a little bit. The city was still illuminated with various fluorescent lights, and the signs still screamed of consumerist, capitalist fodder. I couldn't find any sanctity in it, however, other than drinking irresponsibly for hours on end. The night was now approaching its twilight stages, the time in which the sky begins to move away from a pitch black, to a light blue. I felt a new sense of dread; the type in which I knew that this moment was do or die. If only I had decided to kill earlier. Killing the one woman who had caused so much pain and grief upon my sullen life would renew me. I was desensitized to the idea of murder now. I had gotten away with it before, I now had the sense that this was just one little murder, in the face of many.

I threw and broke the drink bottle on the street. I couldn't care less on any repercussions I would face going forward. The night was soon coming to an end, and the police would find Ricardo in a heartbeat. I walked around aimlessly for another few miles, and when I felt my legs give in, I looked up. It was rather run down in comparison to all the other clubs in the area, but certainly wasn't lacking when it came to filling it up. It was indeed, the 'Honey's Gentleman's Club'. Suddenly, I started gleaming from seemingly nothing. But I knew, this was a massive find. It was a blessing in disguise. This was, indeed, the club where I would find the source of my torture. Meredith.

I couldn't wait any longer. It was there, right in the face. I tried composing myself, for one second. Even in my current state, I could not make any rash decisions. But the mere thought of crossing paths with Meredith again ignited thoughts I could not conceive in my wildest dreams. Upon entry, it was a familiar sight. Poles with girls attached to them like live wires, with men throwing money robotically to appease them. The natural habitat of cucks, as I would say.

I was approached by a rather tall man, who brought back flashbacks to that fateful day. He had the word 'Samoa' tattooed, with a tight-fitting black polo shirt.

"It's last call, so you better be quick" he said, as he gestured for something in the distance. I just needed to find that fucking slut, Meredith and I would be out in a flash.

"Some of the girls have been taken home, so there are only a few I must warn you" he said, as he pulled out a catalogue, as if these girls were items of jewellery for demand by men. They were nothing more than sluts, however.

"Can I take a look?" I said, sheepishly. I had to hope that Meredith was available. She wasn't the best looking, certainly.

He handed me the catalogue, and I viewed all the other sluts that were available for my pleasure. I had no time to be fucking about, so I scanned, until my eyes were met with a familiar sense of lust, as well as disgust. Her eyes were just as I remembered. Those lips, the perfect proportion with minimal blemishes in her overall complexion. She had a simple, yet complex face which was visually appealing to any cuck who laid eyes on her. I could tell from the 'Popular' red label covering a corner of her hair.

"Is this one still here" I said, whilst putting my meaty finger on that slut's face. My heart was pounding, not even committing slaughter was this daunting to me.

"She got taken by some Spanish looking dude, who didn't even fucking pay" he said, as he went slightly off track.

I stopped for one second and took that second to fully process what this Samoan had just said. There was no possible way that Ricardo had done this. Was it even that piece of shit? Something strong in my mind had told me that he had done it. He had indeed taken Meredith from this club. I needed to hand it to him, he was smarter than I had anticipated. But now, I was in a race against time. He turned to Meredith as a source of comfort after his parents abandoned him. I would have never anticipated it, but I needed to accept it and find him. If anything, this outcome would prove better as I could kill both Ricardo and Meredith in one fell swoop. But one thing was for certain, I would not rest until I did find those two. I needed to do it before the police managed to get their hands on them.

THE THRILL OF THE HUNT

"My house is right there" Meredith said, as she pointed to a rusted, green door. She was on edge; I could feel it. She had put on a beige trench coat over her visibly little clothing and moved me out of the way to put the key in the lock.

I could see her hands, teaming with black acrylic nails, shaking. Did she think I was a killer as well?

"How do I know you aren't going to kill me?" she said, before she opened the door.

I emptied my pockets and let her view up and down my body. It seemed like this was enough evidence for her, as she opened the door. She fixed her luscious black hair, as she entered the darkness. Turning on the light allowed me to see a home which only contained the bare necessities. Certainly, more well-kept than Remi's former abode, but not somewhere I would have the privilege of calling 'home'. The back of my mind always had both Remi and the police ingrained in there, but I hoped that Remi had assumed I killed myself. The signs were certainly there.

"You know at 30, I thought I would have my life figured out" she said, as she took a seat on one of the shanty recliners. "Even though I get banged almost every night, I've never felt… fulfilled". She was looking around her house, almost feeling guilty she even brought me here. "I have no purpose in this world, at the end of the day. The pretty face, and large breasts don't help me as you think they do".

"Meredith, listen" I said. "Before my life got screwed, I was heading towards a life of despair, and little purpose. I've graduated college with a degree I'm not proud of in the slightest, and I've been subject to constant jealousy and heartbreak in the face of my peers" I said, as I leaned upon the mould ridden walls. The paint was chipping off in some areas, with the chippings falling onto the grey, stained carpet floor.

Meredith cleared her eyes and looked at me again.

"I don't want to be a slut, I never wanted to" she said, as she broke down in tears. "It's very degrading, when you aren't addressed as human, reduced to a fucking sex object for men's pleasure"

I was a man; I could feel it for once. But what was a man? I spent all this time, trying to rekindle a sense of masculine pride, but seeing a woman break down in tears as a prostitute gave me a new sense of shame that I would even address them as 'sluts.

"Most women my age are mothers. They have something to cling onto, but me? I'm nothing but a tool for men" she said. I knelt beside her and wiped her tears from her eyes. Her eyeliner began to run down her delicate cheeks, yet still retaining her beauty. "My life has been wasted" she said, as my hands were still in her eyes.

I wanted to comfort her, but I was certain I was not the right person for that. Surprisingly, even with her dashing looks and desirable status as a woman, she too felt disconnected from the world.

"I could have been a mother. I could have started a family and felt some sort of fulfilment in the world. I would have people who loved me, and I would love them back. But I just had to become a fucking whore" she said. "Isn't that a big part of being a woman?"

"Listen, Meredith. You are a strong woman. You deserve so much more, but you can't get caught up on what you have and have not done. We all feel like we are behind in something. Seeing people, you grew up with doing things you could only dream of is degrading, but we need to live with it, and look at our own merit" I said. I wasn't the type to give motivational speeches, nor will I be, but I just needed us to be on the same page. I cleared her eyes once more, as I stared directly into them. They were the deepest black, alluring to look into, and admire. I was still staring directly at her. We didn't lose an ounce of eye contact, even though her black eyeliner was beginning to seep into her cheeks. Something came over me in that moment, as I drew closer into her grasp, and could feel the heat radiating from her lips. Eventually, our lips locked as we exchanged a deep ocean of emotions and admiration. I could feel her breathing, with her arm wrapped elegantly around me. I could feel her black acrylic nails dig into my skin as I carried on, without question. We paused for a second, as my head and hers collided. She fixed her luscious black hair and we continued. It must have lasted a while, as her breathing intensified. I wanted to take it a step further, and she allowed it. I had now entered her swamp, her box of discovery.

She certainly had experience; she knew exactly what I wanted in the moment. Her body had the perfect proportions, just enough for me to feel a proper connection. I knew that this was the true essence of love as it radiated off her deep, lust worthy skin.

We were both sweating, as she kept breathing heavily every time I would go in. As we finished, I could only feel confusion, but that renewed sense of purpose. She needed this as much as I did. My sweat did not let up, however as I tried clearing my face, refusing to look back at Meredith as I could feel the rustle of her putting her clothes back on. The room was silent, I was guessing she could tell I felt a sense of guilt from the whole encounter. She had experience, after all.

"I'm guessing I wasn't that great" I said, whilst refusing to look back at her.

"No." she said. "That was, refreshing."

I'm guessing that was her way of telling me I was 'okay'. After the encounter with that prostitute we later killed, I have been critical of my performance. Not that it mattered anyways, I wouldn't have this type of connection from a prison cell.

I was in love, however. But I didn't know how to handle this newfound feeling.

She paused as she was putting her clothes on and tried to get me to look at her.

"Are you, ashamed?" she said, in the softest voice possible.

"No, I'm just… empty." I replied.

I could feel her hand touch my shoulder, she was still completely naked, and I could feel her breasts on my back. I took a breath as I could feel her cold touch and looked back at her. I could feel her hair on my shoulder as she embraced me whole.

"You calmed me down, Ricardo. I'm an emotional person, but the way you handled that satisfied me completely"

She spoke. She clearly didn't know the actual reason I felt so, empty. I should have told her I suffer from sleepless nights now, after having my life screwed by Remi. The police could knock at any second, and that is what truly terrified me. They were only moments away from busting this door open. I directed her hands away from me, as she laid down on the bed, clearly inviting me to lay alongside her. I didn't know what exactly to feel, having a woman naked next to me. It was a new feeling, but one I could not complain about.

"Are you going to spoon me, or what?" she said.

"Well, are you aware that I am a fugitive in fear of my life?" I said, sarcastically. "And not only that, but I also most likely have a psychopath chasing me as well as the police". I certainly was pissed after the pleasure I had just experienced. I couldn't sleep, but I laid down regardless. Her body was inviting, as she wrapped her arms around me. My eyes were wide open, as I looked around the room, the giant tower fan in the centre of the lone bedroom, with photos that displayed the stock images on the wall. It seemed to me that Meredith was lonely despite her profession. She broke down in tears in front of someone she presumed to be a 'killer' just moments ago, and just had sex with someone who showed her a little compassion. We had more in common than I had initially thought.

I looked back at her innocent face, seemingly asleep. She had no idea of the carnage Remi was willing to ensue upon her. I hoped I had explained it well enough, but after seeing her asleep like this, I probably did not.

She was innocent, I was sure of it. Remi failed to see her inner demons and took her at face value, for her body. If I am to encounter Remi again, he would certainly decide to kill me. My body went numb just thinking about that one moment. Every time I would close my eyes, my ears would zero in on every single sound. Even the faint knocking all around the apartment complex. It was yet another night in which I could not sleep, as it had been for the past couple of nights. One would expect me to feel relieved that someone had resonated with me, but I just could not escape the dilemmas that had plagued my life. If I do make it out, what do I even do? I would hope that my mother found out the truth about who killed my father, and I would be able to connect with her once more. For now, I was a dead man to her whilst she mourned in solitude.

I took another glance at Meredith. She forgot to remove the stripper makeup she had applied, with the black eyeliner still carrying the marks of her crying. But the night still carried that element of ease I always sought within it. I glanced at the window, still with paint marks chipping off it. Despite the obvious state of disrepair, the apartment was in, the skyline was immaculate. You could see a good majority of the strip from simply looking down. The city never slept; it was nearing the early hours of the morning, yet still no one looked to be moving. Remi was probably among these people, most likely drinking his sorrows or sleeping with another prostitute. He saw women as sex animals, something to be toyed with.

The police could knock on this door any minute. I kept my eyes now fixated on that rusted thing, with the sound of the clock above it, ticking. Every second that passed, I would hold my breath. This was my life now. It felt like a form of torture, but this was it. Where did I go after this, I did not know.

THE WORLD'S REVENGE

I walked through the night once more. The streets were now much emptier, but the sky was beginning to light up. Ricardo did not commit suicide as I had expected, but he had done something much worse. I was extremely lethargic; the whole night was spent trying to find those two. Those drinks that I had downed a couple hours ago did not help either, my body was now expecting me to rest up for the remainder of the night. But I needed to work faster than the police could, I needed to find that whore and her suitor. Meredith was close, at least. I knew she would be a whore, she deserved nothing less. But Ricardo? He barely spoke to women before, nor did he attract any. I could say the same for myself, but I wasn't exactly a 'moral' individual. I needed to admit, that Meredith was attractive, in some regard. From the moment I first saw her, she caught my eye back when I had some faith in myself. Seeing her for the first time still plagues my memory even now. Her long, flowy hair with her contagious ass smile. I used to fantasise about her regularly, during my college days. I remember her wanting to pursue acting, or so I had heard. I never had the courage to look at her for more than a few seconds, let alone talk to her. I went off only on overhearing her conversations. My stomach would turn every time she would walk in the same direction as me, her stare was the very thing I yearned for, despite dreading looking at her. I knew I was a lovesick bastard, but I had no experience talking to women. I didn't know how they functioned. Knowing what I do now, the only thing I really wanted was to fuck her. Nothing else. There was no such thing as 'love'. There will not be. At least for men, that is. A man only wants physical affections, and that is the only reason he dares to even 'love' someone in the first place. It is now, when I walk the streets of Las Vegas, I see that love is a flawed ideology. A façade for any woman who believes that a man finds pleasure in providing and 'caring' for them. Why did I rape that girl in the apartment? because as a man, I felt the sense of desire, the sense of hunger that is stored deep within any man's body. The feeling of lust is one that cannot be tamed, even for men who are in 'stable' relationships.

My body still felt weak as I roamed, aimlessly. There was no point in walking, I didn't even know where that bitch lived. The night ended, as the bars were hopelessly trying to empty the crowds out, trying to close. 5AM is a rather interesting time, as you would see degenerates waddling out of the clubs with women of the night, alongside people who have fulfilled their sleep quotas. We were all dreamers back in college. We never thought about where we would end up in the next few years, what would happen to our lives. I took a seat next to a giant screen, looking all around. All hope was seemingly lost. I could still see the strip club from here, but it was too late. It was a couple hours away from being 'game over' for me. Once the police find out, I will be found in a matter of minutes. Speaking of the police, I looked toward the strip club right opposite, and soon enough, two police cars were parked up in the small parking lot next to the club. I decided against my better judgement, to walk up to it and observe from afar. I knew that there was a good chance they were talking about Ricardo. Why else would the police be there? It was that time where the streets were beginning to clear out, the people passed out on the streets, and men taking women home. The police could also be there for that reason. I carried on walking up anyways, as I had nothing left to lose.

Both officers looked like they took no prisoners, and stormed themselves inside the building, and to the Samoan who was at the door.

If it was about Ricardo, I knew I needed to act quick.

The sun was beginning to rise, and the club was winding down. I stood relatively near the entrance and covered myself within the crowd that were leaving the place.

"We've had word that Ricardo Joaquin Castillo is here." One of the officers said. It was Ricardo. I knew it. "Could you tell me where he is?" they added. The Samoan started to converse with the other man he had stood next to him and brought a large book.

"He's a Spanish looking guy with glasses, semi muscular build and a small goatee and moustache."

The man immediately knew who he was talking about, and if I could recall, he didn't pay for the girl he brought home.

"He went home with, uh Paradise" he said. I had been proven right once again. He went home with Meredith.

"Where is home?" one of the police officers sarcastically added.

"I don't know" the Samoan replied.

I would expect the police to figure out that the place was no use to them, but they carried on interrogating.

"Give us the girl's address" one of them said. It looked like I could get all the information I needed right here.

"We can't really do that, it's against policy" he said, in a rather cocky tone. The police officers looked like they got impatient, and one of them pinned the Samoan to the wall.

"If you don't give us the fucking address, we will arrest you, and seize any dollars that have been hidden away, so I suggest you co operate sir".

"1406 Bordello Avenue"

"I'm just going to have to ask you a couple questions, and we will be off" one of the officers said.

Shit. I needed to get the hell out of there and get to that address. I had it ingrained in my mind, as I ran past the shitty parking lot, and onto the main road. Ricardo must be there as well. But if I found Meredith, I did not give a shit what happened to him.

I had my gun; it was loaded with 4 bullets. I made sure the safety was off before I scanned around the place. The roads were empty, with the bright yellow and red signs reflecting onto the street. I needed to act quick and get to the address by any means necessary.

I saw an open top Chevvy in the distance, it was one of the only cars that would pass by. I ran to it, whilst concealing my gun. Whoever was in that thing, I didn't care.

As it approached, it looked to be driven by a man with a shaved head, with a visibly pregnant woman in the passenger seat. Quite an odd combination to say the least.

I threw myself in front of the car, and made it grind to a halt.

The man in the front seat was muscular, I could tell. But he was no match for me shooting him point blank.

"What the fuck are you doing?" he said, as he honked at me furiously. I could shoot now, but that wouldn't be ideal, considering that the police were in the vicinity.

I needed to act smart. I couldn't rob the car either, so I made the logical choice of getting inside the car.

"Get the fuck out, fatass" he said as I made myself comfortable. This was a good time to pull out my weapon and I did just that and pointed it at him.

"Listen fucker, I could shoot you and your pregnant hoe in 5 seconds. But I want you to drive up a little bit, up until that stop sign there". Doing this would ensure I could stay hidden from the cops, but I was in a race against the clock. I could not entrust this muscular bald individual to drive me anywhere, so I needed to shoot him, and take control of the car. Or if he complied, it would be better for him. His masculinity was touched by the fact another man was controlling him, and it was pleasurable to see. He looked at the pregnant woman next to him, and she gave him a look of reassurance. Soon enough, he began to drive.

I could hear the man breathing heavily, as he kept his hand on the woman's pregnant belly whilst steering the car. I however, kept the gun fixated on his veiny skull whilst he was driving. It was amazing to see someone cower in fear before me.

He stopped the car in front of the stop sign and kept his hand on his wife's stomach. He looked back to see me, with a glock pointed directly at him, with no sympathy in my eyes.

"Is this where you need to get off?" he said, whilst trembling, and slurring his words. "Please get off" he continued, as he lost every ounce of masculinity inside his body. The pin drop silence didn't help things either, as I didn't utter a word, nor did his supposed spouse.

I didn't get off.

If only he knew what I was going to do, and who I was.

A droplet of sweat oozed down from the woman's neck, as the silence continued. A crescendo of breathing began, as they began to realise who I was.

"Who are you?" the woman added. "Are you that Ricardo guy?" she said, as she may have realised who they let inside their car.

"Please god, no" the 'man' said. He began to cry, as he was contemplating running away. Seeing his tears brought me nothing but joy.

"No, please don't kill us, please" the woman said as her floodgates began to open as well.

"Please don't kill us, we have a child on the way" she said.

"Ricardo, please".

She wished I was that fucking scumbag. I was no Ricardo, and unfortunately, there was no way out for them.

"Get out, you can run." I said to the man, as I lowered my weapon. "Take your wife with you".

I gave them a sense of false hope as the man held his wife's hand and left the car. Their tears had subsided, to a possible sense of relief.

They ran, and I started the car once more, the address was still clear in my head. 1406 Bordello Avenue. I looked at them once more, through the mirrors of the car and I wanted to kill them. The fact that they were going to start a family angered me. It made me sick. Their helpless running was a relief, at least. Seeing them run for their lives gave me a renewed sense of power, as I began to place my foot on the gas, and speed towards the address.

END OF THE ROAD

It is now 5:30 A.M. I still hadn't slept a wink. I didn't even fall into a grace period, in which I would shut my eyes for a faint second before I drifted into slumber. Meredith lived near a rather metropolitan area, I could hear cars and sirens very clearly from the apartment. I would hold my breath until they passed, every single time. I'm not a deranged killer. I would hope that the police understood as I waited for their arrival. I would much rather the police find me than Remi, in which case Meredith would be in danger. I knew I couldn't let that happen. The sun was beginning to rise, as the rays penetrated the window, and blasted into our apartment. There was no turning back. The morning had already come. The hazy sky and baking sun always gave me a renewed sense of hope, but I knew there was none. Being framed for a crime was something I would not wish on my worst enemy, especially since I finally had found someone who I connected with. But deep down, it was only a matter of time before the inevitable would happen.

I could hear some noises coming from downstairs. The place was filled with meth heads and heroin addicts, you could tell from the types of unsavoury characters located in this apartment complex. I could hear droplets of rain beginning to pour as the night began to cross paths with the sun. The sound of the droplets crashing against the window gave me some form of serenity, as it always had.

I could hear the crashing sounds from downstairs getting louder, but I couldn't take the risk of investigating it. I looked toward the door, and braced myself for whatever outcome. I could hear footsteps. The sound of boots colliding in rain puddles in a uniform manner. Every step increased my heart rate. The creaking of the bed didn't help either, the tension was increasing in my mind as well as my ears. The footsteps sounded nearby, clashing with the rain which had now become heavier to the point it drowned out the footsteps.

I shook Meredith's shoulder relentlessly as I needed her to wake up.

"Wake up" I said, continuously. The sounds became louder and came to a halt. I could audibly hear myself breathing, as I refused to get up from this bed. I had a good feeling it was Remi, or the police.

Meredith got up and looked around. Her hair was out of place and her makeup was still on.

Suddenly, I heard a banging noise ringing from the door. My heart rate began to reach unfathomable levels as I looked toward Meredith for some explanation. I hoped this wasn't what I was thinking. But there was a strong chance it was.

I snuck up to the door and peered through the small opening down the middle. I could see two police officers; both wore bulletproof vests with a beige uniform.

They carried on banging on the door, not stopping. They were certainly here for me. Who else would it be?

"Las Vegas Police Department, open this goddamn door" one of them said. They weren't in the mood to be nice either.

Meredith stared directly at the door. So, did I. We both didn't move an inch from the bed, I was too shocked, even though I was building for this moment.

"How the hell did they find us?" Meredith said, as she pulled me closer. She held my hand, despite only knowing her for one night.

"Fuck" I said, softly. This had to be it. The police were going to arrest me.

"We will knock this fucking door down if you do not comply" one of them said from the door. "Open up, now"

They wasted no time, and started tearing the door down, each thunderous bang made my heart race even faster.

"You should hide" Meredith said, as she got up, ready to answer the door.

"I'll take some responsibility" she added.

"No, Meredith." I said back. "you don't deserve this. Let me answer it and get arrested. I'll be able to clear up everything". I felt a sense of fear when I got up, but I knew I had a chance of clearing everything up. Even though the cops seemed to be aggressive in their approach. Meredith obliged and ran inside the laundry room.

"Also, I'll make sure Remi is taken care of, if he comes, just try and distract him" I said as she went into the room. That was if Remi didn't decide to murder her by then.

The door bust open, and the cops stared me directly in the eye. Their badge was on show, a golden star on the ID badge. I knew how this went.

"Ricardo Joaquin Castillo, you are under arrest on suspicion of murder". They spoke. "Hands behind your back".

I went through with it, as they tied me, and took me out of the apartment. I hated being stared at, and it seemed like all the crackheads had turned up to see the arrest.

I held my breath as I was transported, is this really what my 'loving' mother wanted?

The feeling was humbling, being the centre of attention for all the wrong reasons whilst being thrown in the back of a police car.

"Is that comfortable enough for you?" one of the officers sarcastically added. It seems like they wanted to tame their masculinity, by throwing me into the car like this.

They started up the thing and began to set off.

"Make sure he's properly fitted at the back" one of them said. There were only two officers alongside me, both sitting in the front of the car. I looked up at the apartment, as the police car sped off in the rain. You could barely see anything from the windows, as the rain took complete control of the atmosphere. The sound of the rain helped calm me down a bit. I was surprisingly calm as we left the place, knowing that I could rectify all the wrongs, but my main concern was Meredith, and if Remi were to find her. Surely the police realised that Remi was also someone of note in the case.

We went through the city; the lights were shining on my face as the rain made everything blurry. The entire ordeal was something I had tried to anticipate, but I couldn't.

My whole body now needed to cope with some form of numbness as we continued to drive through the city. I never had time to appreciate the skyline, the lights on every street corner, or the glamorous cars dotted on every single street.

I continued to sit there, with a straight face. I looked out, beyond the horizon, and wondered when I would see it again. I did aid Remi in those murders, and I cannot escape him. I had the intention of telling the police exactly who he was, and maybe I could be proven innocent.

THE WORLD'S REVENGE

It seemed like I was fighting a losing battle. Was Ricardo dead? Was Meredith with him?

All these questions would be rampant in my head as I continued speeding down the streets of Las Vegas. The rain was making everything hard to see whilst the wipers worked relentlessly to keep the water from obstructing my view. The buildings in the area looked abandoned, rusted and displaced. Surely that whore was living in an area like this. I had fucked many escorts over the years, and all of them hailed from areas that looked like this. It came as no surprise a slut was roaming around these parts.

This city was one that never ceased to fascinate me; the bright lights and capitalist signals plagued one end of the place yet run down shanty towns encapsulated the other half.

The couple had left a couple hundred bucks in the car, with a sticky note attached to them. It had the word 'Abortion' written on it. Whilst I was excited that they had left some cash inside, I couldn't help but realise what they were trying to do. If only I could procreate with a woman, instead of loathing every single person who lived with a 'happy' family. My parents soon realised what had happened in the apartment I was staying at, and naturally grew worried. But after telling them I had raped a girl; they didn't seem too keen on talking with me again. I didn't see any problem with it, but I naturally knew that rape was frowned upon.

I pulled up to the driveway of the given address. It was hard even for me to believe that Meredith lived in a place like this. The once aspiring actor was now living in a shanty apartment building infested with crackheads and heroin addicts.

Seeing her supposed abode brought me much pleasure. I always held her on a pedestal, during my tragic time at Community College. But seeing men slumped over, administering injections in plain sight made me gleam.

I had no problems locating Meredith's apartment. It was the only one with a white door, whilst the rest were either barricaded or black.

I had my gun alongside me, ready to enact my pleasure. I didn't want to waste my time down here with these sewer dogs, so I swiftly walked over to the dark staircase, just near the foyer.

"I've got heroin" I heard from a voice behind me.

It was a piece of homeless looking scum, holding a plastic injection needle, staring directly at me. I stared back and looked him up and down. He had an untamed beard, with a luminous blue coat. It looked like he hadn't showered in a while, either.

"Want a hit?" he said, as he advanced the injection toward me.

"Fuck you, bum" I said, as I went up the stairs. I could hear some drunken shouting coming from him, but he wasn't worth an ounce of my time. For some reason, I felt more valued here, more important. I could have just barged inside the door, and shot that bitch point blank, but I had nothing to live for. I wanted Meredith's death to cause pain, to cause suffering and outrage. So, I decided to let my inner demons loose, and knock politely on the door.

I kept knocking for a few minutes, to no answer. It seemed that nobody was there to answer, and I was prepared to leave.

But suddenly, in a moment of sheer coincidence, someone answered the door, whilst my back was turned. I could hear the door swing open, and a female voice could be heard.

"Hello?"

I recognised it, how could I not. It was indeed Meredith. But how would I approach her? How would she know who I was?

I acted impulsively and pinned myself onto her doorway. Fuck. She had no makeup on, but still looked visibly attractive. Her facial features aligned perfectly with my beauty standard. I wouldn't expect her to be at a place like this, however. And I was shocked to even see her, as was she.

She tried shutting the door, but I blocked it. I wasn't letting this slip away. My life was a tragedy solely because of her. I fell into a life of crime, and depression because of that bitch. I wasn't letting her go, and I wanted her to know that.

I began to shed tears. Tears that I had never experienced before. I never thought that seeing a senile whore like her would bring me to my weakest point, but if one person made your life spiral into a tragedy, I would expect this exact reaction.

"Who are you?" she said, as I stood there, bawling my eyes out.

"Who the fuck do you think whore" I screamed, as I carried on shedding tears.

I grabbed my gun in a moment of rage, and pointed it at her neck, pushing her back into the shotty apartment she called 'home'.

She fell to the floor and started breathing heavily. I did too. She was dressed exactly how I envisioned her to be. A fucking slut who had no purpose other than satisfy sexual desires.

She soon realised who had entered her shitty home. I closed the door and grabbed my weapon from my pocket. I could kill her right on the spot, but something told me she needed a public execution. Something that would make her death known to the entire world. It was an impulsive decision, but I was willing to go through with it.

"Listen slut. Do you remember when you fucking ruined my life by filing that sexual assault charge?" I said, looking down on her. Not a shred of remorse permeated from her eyes. Why would it? Not even when a gun was pointed at her face.

"Remi, you invaded my privacy when you did that. I felt, harassed, and violated."

I laughed in her face. This was a laughable scenario. She was a prostitute, a woman who carried no purpose, other than to submit to a man's sexual desire. My laughter was justified, whilst she looked mortified.

"You aren't a respected member of society, Meredith. You are a second-class citizen. A fucking whore who's only job it is to give lap dances to men who aren't happy with their lives. Don't tell me you have fucking privacy, because you don't"

"Remi, I was young then" she said. "I have hopes and dreams too".
"And now you are a dirty whore on the streets of Vegas." I spoke. I could not believe she was mouthing off to me after I explained my tragic suffering to her.

"That dream was to give blowjobs for twenty bucks" I said, in a snarky manner.

The gun was still pointed at her face, but she grew used to it being there. Her eyes were still petrified, just what I wanted.
The rain was still crashing against the window, tearing apart the scenic skyline.

"Do you think I ever wanted to live here, let alone work as a stripper, going home with guys every night?" She said, as tears started running from her eyes.

"I would imagine that is the best career path for you" I said, as I began to light a cigarette. "What happened to your little Samoan boyfriend?" I said, as I struggled to light the thing.

"He was the one who brought me here" she said, as she wiped the tears from her eyes.

"I wanted to pursue acting, and he knew that. He was a couple years older than both of us, but he said he had connections. I didn't believe him at first, but after my parents lost everything after college, I was desperate for a lot of cash to keep us afloat. I told him, and well he offered to take me here. I was, alone. And he took advantage of that. He sold me numerous times to be raped, assaulted and starved until I started working at the gentleman's club." She said. "I'm still being exploited, and I keep very little of the money. Do you think I want to live amidst a ton of meth heads?"

I carried on pointing the gun toward her. My struggle with women was far greater than what she had said.

"Have you got some alcohol, at least?" I spoke. Smirking.

"It's in the fridge."

I tossed the cigarette butt on the floor and opened the fridge, still seeing her as I pointed the gun at her. She had some cheap stuff, but it was probably enough to get me drunk. I popped it open and started chugging it down, with no regrets.

"So you had to come up with a sob story just for me to not kill you?" I said, as I kept focus on her.

"Then why else would I be here?" she replied, with vigour.

"Do you know what I went through?" I looked at her whilst saying it. "I couldn't get a fucking stable job when they found out I was a sex offender. And what pissed me the fuck off was hearing your shitty profession after I had gone through so fucking much. I could have lived a fulfilled life by now, but you screwed me over" I said. Those were the words I was waiting to scream out ever since seeing she became a stripper.

"I could have as well" she said, as she got up and sat down on her shitty bed.

"I'm 30 fucking years old Remi. I could have started a family, could have a dignified career, but my poor life choices led to this. You need to take accountability as well"

I couldn't care less about what she had said, I only knew that my life was spoiled, because of her. I looked around the room properly, and I saw something that caught my eye. It was a suitcase; the same one Ricardo had taken when he escaped from my company.

"Who's fucking suitcase is that whore?" I said, putting my drink down. I knew the answer, I just wanted to see her own up.

"It's mine" she said, as her eyes switched between me and the suitcase. It clearly wasn't hers. Her tone of voice sounded worried and agitated.

"That fucker Ricardo was here, wasn't he?"

I wanted more details, but that rat probably told her everything she needed to know.

"So what?" she said, now sounding more cunning than she ever was. "He's with the police. He's innocent"

I always knew Ricardo was a fucking cuck, and it showed. The way she talked about him angered me, seems like she was in love with the guy already.

I smashed the drink bottle on the floor and pinned her against the wall. I felt her breaths go from loud to heavy. I had the gun placed against her throat, as my chest could feel her body.

"You fucked him, didn't you"?

Quite typical for someone of her type.

"I can't believe you would frame someone like that." She said, as she was choked up against her shitty wall. "He was scared. You ripped him from his mother, killed his father and now you suddenly care about him?"

She clearly didn't know the reason I used Ricardo in the first place. "Listen bitch. I became friends with Ricardo, I thought he was someone who shared the same sentiment as me, someone who was headed in the same direction as me. I felt a moral duty to save him from ever having the feeling of 'love'. It doesn't exist." I said, still pinning Meredith against the wall, silencing whatever she was going to say.

"Especially if you were someone like us. He didn't speak to me for months before he came begging for help after his parents kicked him out. I saw, opportunity. He clearly didn't understand my way of thinking, so I killed a prostitute in front of him." I said, as she let out an audible gasp, shocked at what I had said.

"I soon realised, that having two people was better than one, and I was set on completing my final act. Which is to slaughter you." I smiled, as she came to terms with my words.

"And what's better is, it's all gone to plan. I don't give a single fuck that Ricardo is going to tell the police my fucking biography, I have you right where I need you."

I was satisfied at the prospect of saying those words. All those years of suffering, being labelled a 'pervert' had come full circle. I knew that this was going to be my final act, but I didn't expect it to be filled with this much joy.

"Ricardo can't meddle with this now. He's not going to save you. Hopefully he can save your dead body once I'm finished with you." I tapped her soft cheek and yanked her with me.

She screamed, but I didn't care about the consequences at this point. It was time.

It was time to relieve those years of suffering.

I threw her into the stolen Chevvy and closed the door. I felt a slight tap on my shoulder, and I yanked my gun, ready to shoot.

"Want some heroin?" I heard.

It was yet another homeless bum. I pushed him into the artificial bushes next to the parking lot, and relished in the deep rain, pouring from all angles.

I knew exactly where I was taking her, and where to dispose of her body. The ideal scenario was one where I didn't get caught and could live my life out in sanctity. But I had already come to terms with the fact that there was a strong chance I would be in a cell. For all the slaughter, and the heinous sexual acts I had committed, even I knew I deserved it.

TIME

"We've got to change the booking station" I could hear from the front as we were speeding past in heavy rain.

"Why" The one driving asked.

"He's classed as a violent criminal, we have to go back around, and take him to a larger facility. High Desert State Prison, to be exact." He sounded disappointed, as made a 180 turn in the junction to go back around. Did they not know I could also hear them from the back? The officer driving now had a pissed off face, especially towards his colleague.

"Don't look at me like that. The chief is gonna be on our asses if we don't transport this guy right. So, if you value your mothafuckin' job, don't do that shit". Seems like he caught on.

"Don't you think that old sack of shit could have told us before we started driving?" he said, as he drove the other way.

"Just keep driving" he said.

These handcuffs were killing me in the back, whilst the officer in the passenger seat was playing with the keys in his hands. My hands were buried in the car seat, making the ordeal even more uncomfortable.

"We are taking you to another facility you piece of shit" one of the officers said from the back. I could clearly hear them; they didn't need to say anything.

I agreed, as I tried to make out where we were. The rain completely drenched the window and carried on pressing against it with vigour. We eventually made it to a freeway, I could tell by the rain droplets now flashing past us instead of gracefully pattering on the window's surface.

"Faster you fucking moron" I could hear from the front.

"I'm going fast, just shut the fuck up" one said in return.

We picked up some speed, as the handcuffs squeezed my hands onto the seat even more. The rain still made things hard to see, but I could make out just enough.

I noticed a car, slowing down when it came near us. I could hear the deposit of rain splash as it came nearer to us.

Suddenly, I could see the car getting closer to us to the point it wasn't in its lane anymore. It was directly next to us.

It rammed the side of us, immediately catching the attention of both officers. It rammed us again, this time we heard a large thud on the side of the car.

I tried looking out, but I kept reeling from the force of the other car.

"Dispatch, we have a situation" one officer said, in worried fashion. "Keep fucking driving, kee-"he said, as he felt the car ram into us even harder. The driver was struggling to keep the police car straight, as it swerved across the road.

It couldn't be, could it?

I tried my best to peer out of the window, I needed to see who was driving this car. As he drew closer to ram us once again, I saw it.

Fuck. Fuck. Fuck.

It was him.

"Dispatch, can you hear us, we are being attacked on the road" the officer in the passengers' seat said, as he was also looking feverishly to catch the licence plate of the car. "It's a Chevrolet bla-"

He rammed us once again.

We swerved all across the road, to the point the car completely turned around.

I tried to make out what had just happened, but I saw a large beacon of white plague my eyes, with only one man visible.

Remi Palludan.

I passed out for a faint second, and once I regained consciousness, I could feel a trail of blood drip from my forehead. I was breathing heavily, wallowing in what looked to be broken glass, with rain seeping inside the car's interior. One thing I did recognise, was the keys that had now ended up on my seat after all the commotion. I grabbed them, and untied myself, relieved of all the pain I had been subject to since my arrest.

I looked around; it was just me who survived it seemed. The other two officers were covered in blood, with glass burrowed deep in their faces. They were not going to make it.

"Get the fuck out of the car Ricardo" I could hear from outside.

Shit. He knew that I was going to make it out alive.

I felt like playing dead, but I had enough of Remi's fucking voice. I felt a rare sense of confidence, as I crawled out of the wreckage, and onto the wet highway, which had now been halted by Remi.

It was exactly what I had feared. This was the scenario that would play in my nightmares, if I were to get any sleep.

He had Meredith, in a chokehold in the middle of the highway.

I immediately needed to get up, and stop this fucker, for the final time.

"I thought this bitch deserved a far grander ending than most of my victims" he said, laughing maniacally. "Right in front of you".

He had the gun pointed to her head, ready to shoot whilst I cautiously walked closer to him.

"Looks like your time is also up, Castillo." He said in front of the whole highway, with rainwater entering his mouth. "You served me well."

He knew I couldn't fight. And he relished in seeing my face, full of shock, and hatred.

Meredith was kneeling on the ground, begging for her life, whilst he stood there, laughing whilst gripping her arms tight.

I clenched my fists, breathing heavily. Remi saw this.

"What are you gonna do, big boy? Fight me?" he said, as he carried on laughing.

"Where did you find her" I said.

He stopped laughing for a second. "Well, the police were useful for once, and gave me this whore's fucking house, isn't that, right?" he said, as he made her head splash onto the road.

I kept breathing heavily. I immediately remembered that woman on the train. I couldn't do anything but watch. Would I let that happen to Meredith?

"Leave her alone" I said, firmly.

"But she's the love of my life" Remi said, sarcastically. "You will really enjoy when I blow her brains out, Ricardo."

I needed to charge at him, or else I would see something much more horrific than my face being shredded to bits.

"I knew you weren't a fucking man, Ricardo. Look at you. You had sex with her, and you're standing there like a pussy." He punched her in the face once more, as she screamed for help.

Why was I frozen? My ears began to zone out, only hearing echoes of speech, and loud car horns urging us to wrap up our feud. I could hear my breathing clearly. I looked around. This was what my life had come to. Face to face with a psycho, about to kill a woman who I loved.

"Come on Ricardo, show us you aren't a failure"

It was an impulsive decision, as I jumped headfirst on top of him, giving my best attempt at wrestling him to the ground. The gun he wielded, shuffled across the road, as I carried on trying to pin him down. I could see his face, surprised I had made it to this point. Guys would try and fight me in high school, pinning me down in this exact position to show their dominance. I knew I was doing something right, at least. In that moment, he managed to pull my hair and punch me, several times in the face, whilst swapping positions with me to properly dent my skull. It didn't compare to the beatings I received in high school. It was of a much more sinister nature. Despite the impending devastation I was likely going to face, I felt relieved, in some odd sense. I stopped him from taking the gunshot, at least.

The gun went underneath the car's wreckage, stopping anyone from claiming it. Meredith was lying on the road, unconscious from the punches. He laughed as he carried on bloodying my face, landing more thunderous blows in rapid succession. My hands did nothing to protect me, as blood kept visibly gushing out of me. He began to laugh, uncontrollably as more hell rained upon me.

"I'm going to kill you with my bare fists you fucking cuck", he said it with seriousness as he landed some more.

It was at this point; I began to come to terms with my death. Those harrowing punches I was receiving from him, were soon going to stop, I believed. Meredith was not coming to her senses, and I, a hapless lover, got punished for her safety.

"Come on Ricardo, save your fucking mistress". He was taunting me, as he carried on his assault.

"You are going to die now". He said. It played in my head. All those childhood memories, my blank slate into this sullen, unforgiving world was now coming to an end. I could feel my breathing, the individual breaths felt like gold as Remi stepped away. He went to retrieve the gun from underneath the car wreckage. I glanced at my hand; those bloodstains were a reminder of my false manhood.

I closed my eyes, for a faint second, anticipating the bullet. I could hear him getting it ready. The world around me turned silent. The cold, unforgiving world.

I heard the gunshot. Clenched my fists for one final time, in dire anticipation of the wound, the blood emptying out from the hole the bullet had created, the familiar sound of the thud when it hit.

Yet I could open my eyes. Granted, I didn't want to.

The pain I felt after those indescribable thuds from a psychotic killer would only make me die quicker. Until I heard a scream in the distance.

"You fucking, you, you fucking whore"

I arose from my supposed eternal slumber, and saw Meredith, with bloodstains on her corset, and heavy breathing.

She had shot him.

I cleaned some remnants of the blood from my mouth and face as I could only manage to sit down on the wet road. I had been beat to a pulp regardless. I couldn't feel my face.

My joints had little motion, my legs felt deflated, for that encounter was something closer to the feeling of death, rather than being beat. But Remi was still alive, although he had little time left. I grabbed my chest, and Meredith helped me up.

The whole road went silent. It was a silence I had never experienced before. Remi bashed his fists on the side of the road, as he carried on breathing heavily.

"My life has been fucking wasted" he said, crying and screaming at the same time. "I'm nothing more than a burden to this world". He said, as the whole road was in shock.

"How fitting, that I am about to die next to the two people who have ruined my fucking life" he said.

"Give the fucking gun to me" I said to Meredith.

Remi was still breathing heavily, his face drenched from the rain.

"You're killing me? It doesn't change the fact that your mother doesn't know you anymore. You are nothing but a disappointment. Your father hated you, Ricardo." He was still breathing heavily as he was losing blood.

"So go ahead, slaughter me. I'll rest easy, knowing you will rot in a cell for the rest of your sad existence". He started laughing, as I withheld the urge to pull the trigger.

I could hear sirens in the distance, the police had arrived.

"Las Vegas Police, hands in the air, both of you" I could hear from a bullhorn. I looked and saw both of us surrounded by cops. Remi was still laughing; with the little life he had left. I paid no attention to the police orders; I kept my gun fixated on Remi. I could see an ambulance had come for him. The possibility of him being saved.

"Hands in the air, now" they said. "We will shoot you"

My breathing intensified, as I could feel myself shaking the gun, but I could not let Remi live. The stretcher had come out, to aid his body. I could feel a spotlight on us from the helicopter in the sky, so I needed to end this quickly.

"Hands in the air, NOW" "We will open fire"

"You are under arrest"

I fired one, then fired one more. The medic screamed in panic, as I emptied the entire barrel on his sorry ass.

Remi Palludan is dead.

I threw the gun on the floor, but it was too late. I felt a sharp sense of pain coupled with numbness. No. No. No.

I tried to touch my back, to see what damage had been dealt. It surely couldn't be life threatening?

Meredith screamed.

I collapsed.

I felt the shockwave of the rain as my head crashed against the road. The blood, gushing out of me made it clear that these, were my final moments as well. It couldn't be, but my mind was certain of it. The same way my mind would force me to do irrational things, the same way my mind chose not to stop Remi earlier.

That same, sullen mind.

Something told me this was my destiny. To die a death shrouded in tragedy, with my story unable to be heard, unable to be uttered in my own words. I wanted to live.

I wanted to. It didn't mean I would.

Time stopped as I saw the police surround me, with Meredith screaming in agony. Was I going to die?

Fuck. The pain was getting worse. I tried to control myself, but I could feel my consciousness slip away. Was this it?

Breathing, you need to control your breathing. I was losing blood at a rapid pace. It was on my back.

My mother, she needed to believe I was innocent. She needed to see me once again. I couldn't die here. No. I won't. No.

I won't die today.

EPILOGUE

CASE NO. 9281
RICARDO JOAQUIN CASTILLO

AFTER THE SUSPECT DID NOT COMPLY, POLICE WERE INSTRUCTED TO USE DEADLY FORCE, WHICH ENDED UP KILLING HIM ON THE SCENE.

Dear Sal Locatelli,
Ricardo Joaquin Castillo was apparently innocent. We just wrapped up the last interview with the girl who was also at the scene. Her name was Meredith Catherine Brown. She said that the guy Castillo shot used him as a pawn in a large-scale operation to try and kill her specifically. I thought the story was hard to believe, but it's up to the judge. But the camera footage, and information we did know makes her story a little more believable.
She also claimed that Palludan was the guy who killed those guys down at Peace Waters all those years ago, but that is probably a dilemma for another day. We did some DNA swabs on the truck that was stolen, and sure enough, Remi Palludan's DNA came up positive, alongside Ricardo's.
Could you get back to me, and we can progress this investigation further with this information.

Also a further note – we cannot ask Ms. Catherine Brown to come in for any more interviews, she's pregnant. With Castillo's child.

Regards,

Officer 8191

ACKNOWLEDGEMENTS

Cover art and further depictions were illustrated by Ruben Chandler

Thank you to everyone who has and had shown me support throughout the writing process. Everyone's support was exactly what spurred me on to carry on writing this story. The book started from seemingly nothing, and to believe I trusted myself enough to create something that would hopefully resonate with a lot of people is something I will always be proud of. My only hope is that the reader has enjoyed reading this story as much as I did, writing it. Once again, my gratitude is eternal, and hopefully we can meet again.

Naweed Abawi

THE LESSER MAN

This is a work of fiction. Names, characters and events are all purely fictitious, and any resemblance to actual events or people, living or dead are purely coincidental.

Printed in Great Britain
by Amazon